PAUL BLAND

THE

WINTER SHAKER

Elm Leaf Publishing

New York, NY

First Printing

All characters appearing in this work are fictitious. Any resemblance to real persons, living or dead, is purely coincidental.

ISBN # 978-0-692-92586-7

PUBLISHED BY ELM LEAF PUBLISHING

New York, NY

Printed in the United States of America

"Yes, I'm a great believer in angels."

(Mother Ann Lee)

The book is dedicated to the many Shakers who gave

their lives for their belief.

Prologue

———————

The setting of this book is New England and New York State, during the 1880s. America in ways both personal and economic, had well-recovered from the terrible results of the American Civil War. Yet, this war that had ended in 1865 with the surrender of the Confederate States, remained as a shadow over the land. With the passing of days and years, it had become "history" as we call it. A solemn memory that remained each season and on every day of celebration or grieving. With the signs of prosperity and a new democratic unity, the young country found its' way. In rural fields and in the streets of the cities of America, there was a new beginning.

Time had moved forward and the freshly wall-papered rooms of houses with new gas lights and Victorian trim had replaced the faded past. It was the Victorian age, the Gilded Age and the Industrial Revolution; all identifying labels as describing the era as inventive, prosperous and with a distinct style. It was the husband and father, the brother and the son that lead a male-dominated world of new commerce and opportunity. Within society, women held their place in the household beneath men, and yet, they found ways of expression through their own remarkable abilities in many things. The female was unquestionably indispensable, although yet, not considered equal to men.

This is a book of fiction and although I have tried to recreate the Mount Lebanon, New York Shaker village as a setting, as it was, like the descriptions of weather and seasons, some of the setting's details were created by the author as suppositions to what might have been. They are also meant to represent a larger place, young America and this post-Civil War era. The brilliant author of this time, Herman Melville, wrote novels with the sea as their setting. The American landscape seemed what was left to me to write about and describe.

The Shakers did not reflect upon fictional writing and preferred literature that was factual and useful in its' instruction of learning. Yet, there was always an element of drama with the Shakers and their history. I have described the characters and their attachment to the physical setting of the novel and the changing seasons, with this idea in mind. The fictional and dramatic reflected best in God's creation.

Throughout the writing of this novel, I have always been aware of how the Shakers strived for perfection in everything they did; in spiritual activity, purpose and industry. Unlike, the secular society outside of their communities, Shaker men and women played more equal roles. They were not a part of mainstream America in action or identity and often, seen as odd and even a threat to traditional society and values with their communal and celibate way of life.

There were less than 300 Shaker members at the Mount Lebanon Shaker Community during this time in the 19th century. The Shaker members were divided into Church families, North and South. There had been a decline in members over the past several decades and for this reason, workers had been hired to help in the tasks relating to economic invention. The economic prosperity of the Shaker's had not been forwarded and the future of the Shaker community was always uncertain. At Mount Lebanon, there was a large property to maintain including land and buildings. The hired help might be farmers, gardeners, carpenters, broom makers or simply unskilled manual workers. There was the conscious idea of an outside world where material possessions and the pace of industry determined much of human activity. This community needed to thrive and make a monetary profit and it was their greatest similarity to the secular world.

I hope this novel gives the reader an image of the Shakers as unique in their great and lasting contribution to America. Not only in the things that they made, including some of the finest examples of innovative American architecture, but also in their example as spiritual activists. Their influence on American culture has been immense. Looking back, never has a group of individuals seemed more American in their manifestation and self-creation.

At this present day, The Shaker workrooms at Mount Lebanon, New York are silent and empty, yet the legacy of the Shakers remains. This Appalachian area is rich in natural resources and is a place of vibrant seasons, Indian spirits and tales of American folklore. It is a land of illuminated valleys and shadowed woodland. It is scenic and yet it also holds a revelation. Here on a pitch-black night, Mother Ann Lee, the leader of the Shaking Quakers rode in a horse drawn carriage to New Lebanon, New York. Near this town, the Mount Lebanon community of Shakers will eventually prosper under the vision of their lord and savior, Jesus Christ. It is meant to be a utopian place of hope and renewal, where good will triumph over evil, in preparation of the Lord's final judgment on earth.

I

The Journey

Boston Massachusetts 1887

It was at the very start of the fall season, before a winter that would be bitter cold for the New England States. Cyryl Megalos, the son of Greek immigrants and now in his twenties, continued to look for a clerk position in the city of Boston. He wore a new suit of clothes. He had brought with him a letter of reference from his employer. In his breast pocket were this and a folded piece of paper on which to write his name and address, if requested to do so. He had also brought along an instrument of writing that needed the ink of an ink well. He would have brought this as well, but he wasn't sure of the necessity as an office would surely have the provision of this.

He now entered an establishment that was connected to the buying and selling of residential and commercial property.

"Hello, I have come to inquire about work in your company," said Cyryl.

"What kind of work? I know that we haven't any job openings at this time," said a man dressed in a dark striped suit and a silk tie.

"I would accept any reasonable position or with the title of office clerk. I have brought a reference from my most recent employer, having worked there in the capacity of an office clerk," said Cyryl.

The man looked at Cyryl's letter of reference with *The Doverman Fishing Company*, as the letter head and then he handed it back to him.

"Very nice reference; and can you read and write?" asked the man. "It says in your letter of reference that you can read "sufficiently to understand instructions to work tasks," said the man.

"Yes, *sufficiently*, sir," said Cyryl, emphasizing the word. "I can write as well, but I have not been in the habit of doing so much writing as reading," said Cyryl.

"For any clerk position here, you would have to both read and write quite proficiently," said the man. Seeing Cyryl's face turn to a look of discouragement, he then added these words.

"I will take your name and address and if something comes up, I will call you," said the man. "It is not likely to happen soon, though, as we have just hired a man to do our inventory books and regular office tasks. You might do yourself a favor and apply at mills or factories that need office clerks. Establishments of that kind need men to run errands and unload merchandise along with clerical duties. It is just a suggestion," said the man.

That day, Cyryl inquired at other Boston companies and at mills and factory offices. Yet, he was greeted with the same response. He lacked experience and "literacy skills," as one woman in an office had put it. When asked about his previous work to The Doverman Fishing Company offices, he confessed that he had been a fisherman and a sailor; framing the experience as hard work and "solidifying his character," and rewarding him "acquirement of self-discipline." This was the response he had decided upon if asked such a question.

Cyryl's view of himself had changed since working in an office. He was proud of his new clerk position and it became an important part of his identity. He was no longer a fisherman but a man attached to a professional workplace on land. It befitted him, he thought. He no longer had to return home exhausted and smelling of fish and salt water. His hands healed as best they could. The redness in his face from long days in the sun went away and his natural skin color returned, as if his own true character had as well. The offices where he worked were clean, neat and organized. It was an attachment to a world he had never experienced before and he was grateful to have found such a position. He thought of his parents and how proud they would be of him. He would not look back but continue with this type of work. He worked hard and he tried to learn all he could, despite his lack of good English and his limited reading ability.

Yet, his new circumstances did not last. Cyryl's office work with The Doverman Fishing Company would end soon. The company had been sold. Cyryl's position as an assistant clerk had been a temporary one. He was welcome to continue as a fisherman as he had previously to his office job, but he did not want to do this. He felt he could not look back. Those painted idyllic and placid scenes of the American landscape that he had seen at the Boston Museum had made him dream of a life on land, away from the coastal docks and the sea. He feared that if he remained in Boston that he would again, be forced to return to life as a fisherman. He had looked for another situation in Boston. He had found nothing; at least, not right away. His meager savings would not allow him to be unemployed for an extended time. With the increase in salary from this clerk position, he had bought a fine suit of clothes and a pair of new shoes. It had taken most of his savings. It was an investment in his future.

His supervisor, Mr. O'Malley was sympathetic to Cyryl's employment circumstance, but he suggested that he fish until something else came along. Cyryl Megalos feared "something else" would never happen and he grew agitated. He had discussed all of this with his good friend, Stephen Blome, who stilled worked as a fisherman. They had worked alongside each other before Cyryl had started his work in an office. Not always in the same fishing vessel, but nevertheless following the same routine of very early mornings and a walk back from the docks to the area in which they lived.

Having found no work, Cyryl grew more discouraged. It was now late afternoon. He reached the corner of a Boston street and looked down its' viewpoint. It was all but deserted in human activity with those residing there, indoors. There were shadows across one side of it, where the buildings blocked the sinking sunlight. A part of it blurred in the daylight as if a dream of somewhere else. It lay empty of promise.

The following day he continued his search. The early morning sunrise was a shade of pink in the sky. Once the dark of night lifted, the buildings of Boston reappeared in the gilded morning light. Gray shadows still covered sections of the edifices and streets. Its' citizens were approaching, attending to their trades and conversing as to their plans, actions, thoughts on commerce, family and the usual chatter of gossip often influenced by a Boston newspaper. There was Chauncy Street, Columbia Street, Essex Street; Brattle Square. These names now familiar to Cyryl.

The Boston city streets evoked its' history. The styles of architecture as seen in the structure of the facades; their windows and doors placed in a set manner. Noise and movement probably much the same as the previous century. The shadows opaque. The sunlight reaching beyond stone cornices to create patterns of angular light onto the stone streets. You represented the era, much the same as any man or woman or child might have, in a previous age. Your needs conventional and with the same mortal limitations.

Seen in the windows of the storefronts, were the activities of the day. The selling of books and fabrics; teas and spices. Great quantities of things bought as a necessity or to be used in the manufacturing or fashioning of another useful item. There was an assumption of survival here. Yet, it was only sustainable with consistent effort.

It was sometimes at day's end, that the shadow that you cast seemed more real than your own entity. But it was only fatigue or a discouraged heart that had brought you to that thought. The evening shadows would go with the night and the morning would bring another day of hope and a new-found direction.

The new day was ahead of him and the prospect of introducing himself to many strangers who appraised him on his dress and speech. He would wait for places of business to open. And then after what he thought was an appropriate amount of time, he would enter and inquire about work. He had learned from his earlier life, that the timing of his actions was important. An opportunity missed or his appearance an intrusion on those around him. Yet, his initial appearance seemed to please others, if only because he was fair in appearance and very polite.

It was now afternoon. Cyryl thought of his friend Stephen on the sea fishing with the others. The work was arduous and sudden; the heavy fishing nets being pulled, in weather different on any given day. Some areas of coastal sea considered dangerous for fishing and the amount of fish always scarce unless you went further out and farther away from the safety of land.

He had been with friend Stephen in all seasons. When it had snowed and they had bundled up against the artic-sent air. In summer heat, when he had been lazy in his attire, preferring the light cotton shirts with sleeves that could be easily rolled up. He had dressed up once or twice, when it seemed necessary, putting on a jacket of wool and a collarless shirt of light yellow cotton. He felt he knew Stephen like no one else and it was probably so.

He looked down a Boston Street not sure of where to go next and for a moment, there seemed nowhere to walk to and so he paused to look at the town about him. The street seemed commonplace and he contemplated nothing, really. It was his future he was searching for. He then began his pace onward to the next place of business. He searched most intensely but to no avail until the shops and factories began to close for the evening. He had no offers to tell of to his friend Stephen.

"Have you found some other work?" asked Stephen, seeing Cyryl waiting at his door.

"No, not yet, but I hope to have something soon," said Cyryl. His face held a look of grave concern. "I will not go back to fishing."

"I work as a fisherman. It is an honest living," said Stephen. "You can work alongside me as before." He gave Cyryl a slight push on the shoulder.

Cryrl thought his decision to not return to work as a fisherman was starting to separate them as friends. Stephen accepted his life as a fisherman. It was an adequate living and it took a certain character of a man to be a fisherman or a sailor. If people looked down on him because of his profession, they were snobbish and stiff shirts. It was always like this. The working-class people at odds with the upper classes who had wealth and position and gave so little to the working-class in the form of wages and fairness in society.

"You are a better fisherman than me, said Cyryl, appealing to Stephen's self-esteem. It's no good for me," said Cyryl. "I prefer the work in an office."

"You'll have to go back to it soon, if you find yourself not working at all and the room's rent is due. A man must work and sometimes at things he does not want to do," said Stephen.

14

"I know this," said Cyryl. "It is not the hard work. It is the type of work I no longer care for. If it were work on land, I would not mind as much. I should be able to find something else in Boston," said Cyryl. It was his plan of self-improvement that he would have to forfeit, if he returned to fishing.

Cyryl had made a good effort and the discontent in his own failure to find employment, showed in his face. He was wearing his best suit of clothes. In his pocket was the reference he had been given by his supervisor at the fishing company, now a bit crumpled from having been opened and folded many times. He had taken the afternoon off at the fishing company to look for work and he would not be paid for those hours missed. It had not been the best of days for him.

"Come on," said Stephen. "I'll treat you to dinner."

"No," said Cyryl, at first, but after Stephen had coaxed him a bit, he smiled and accepted his offer.

"Ok, but I will treat you next, once I find a new office position," said Cyryl.

The cobblestone streets of Boston, Massachusetts, were often narrow and many of the city buildings built during the century before; structures of red brick and stone from New England quarries that had been carved and placed to edge these buildings of revolutionary war history. Their completion representative of the prosperity and human effort put forth by this young country, America.

In spring and summer, the city seemed a pleasant place and its' parks and gardens were green and full of color. When it snowed in the city of Boston, it seemed to make it more somber. The snow still on hats and coats to be swept off as one entered an abode or a place of trade. There, unnoticed at first. A reminder of nature's effect.

The windows of buildings were warmly lit from inside and that is where you wished to be on a gray winter's day. It was a city of trade, a seaport and during the winter months, the sea looked dark and cold and the coastal sea wind made it frigid in temperature and a harsh view to look upon. You bundled up against it, both in the covering of wool and cotton, but also in spirit and soul, for it took a piece of it, if allowed. Once inside, and warmed by a fire and a meal of baked beans or a

15

steaming baked potato, you forgot the bitter weather and remembered you were still strong in physicality. Life was good and brought both cold and heat and the usual circumstances required to survive.

It was the first day of October. The weather was chilly and damp that morning. It had rained and leaves, green and yellow had fallen from the trees. Cyryl's work at the fishing company was to end soon. He had not found another job as an office clerk in a Boston company. He had been a sailor for a time and he had experienced life at sea. He then had decided to be a fisherman like his father had been, along the New England, American coast. It was an uncertain time for him. He wasn't at all sure what his future held.

He thought of his years as a fisherman and a sailor. The New England coastal sea was rough and deep. It had a nature of its' own that was separate from the land in apparition. Its' sound an ancient echo. Its' wet sea-spray salty. When it went up against you with great waves, you could find yourself adrift. Or defeat it by reaching land or riding its' fury. On days when the sun never touched it, its' white waves were contained within the sea itself. Then it was only one color of sea green, lifting and translucent.

The sea was an unknown place, even if you had sailed upon it with a compass or had fished its' salty waters for a lifetime. Its' size not within human conquest. Its' color and shape apart of the sky and constellations. It was old and a reflection of the sun and moon. There to remind you of time and the size of your life.

Above the sea as on land, the sky was different on any given day. White clouds and blue sky or gray clouds, with hues at the horizon. The sky a prediction of rain. Or with a soundless cloud-cover that foretold snowfall. Once you were away from land, you viewed it differently. It was closer to you now, the sky. It could bring life or death; prosperity or ruin.

In a storm on the great deep sea, the one thing that you felt was small and sometimes lost. Most certainly vanquished if you forgot that you had a soul. That you were a believer of holy salvation, as you had interpreted it for even a sinner like yourself. For within that, was a hope born of spiritual strength, that was drawn from something outside of your physical being. It kept men alive, or at death it was a comfort.

16

Cyryl thought of the lighthouse he had seen one afternoon along the New England coast, when it had stormed fiercely and the fisherman had ventured too far from land in search of a better catch. Its' light had been piercing and bright; its' beacon lighting the gray sky then shifting down towards the restless surface of the sea. It might have been at that moment that he had decided he no longer wanted to be a fisherman. How dark the scene had seemed before him. The sound of the fog trumpet. The barely discernable signal of light. The turbulent sea water around him with no apparent horizon. There were flashes of lightning in the sky. The lighthouse in the distance, anchored on land; secure and sound in its' structure and purpose. He had felt misplaced at that moment. A man in need of salvation and without the rudiments of steady living.

In this fierce storm, he had lost his balance more than once while standing in the boat, almost falling into the sea. The fishing boat nearly capsizing and sea water filling its' bow. Many men had lost their lives navigating these seashores filled with rocks. It was difficult to see in the rain and it was the fishermen's purpose to reach a place along the shore where their boat might safely rest and the men escape the rough waters and pouring rain.

It had come upon them, this tempest, as if all at once. They had been too slow in recognizing its' powerful force. It was the edge of something much fiercer, that of a hurricane a farther distance out at sea. But it had moved inland quickly, taking the fishermen off guard and disrupting what had been a good day of fishing and a better profit. The sky above was a terror he had never witnessed. The storm had brought night and the darkest clouds ever seen with a fisherman's eyes. They had escaped with their lives but only after a terrible struggle to guide their fishing boat to safety, with the luck of finding a place to bring the boat and crew ashore.

Cyryl had looked at Stephen sitting on the shore, as if making sure it was indeed his friend. He looked pale and shaken; his clothes sopping wet.

"You look as if I am a ghost," said Stephen, who had thrown himself down onto the grass-covered ground to rest.

"We might all of us have been ghosts!" said Cyryl, breathing heavily from the effort of helping to tow the fishing boat onto land.

"Old Henry saved us. Somehow he knew the shore line." said Stephen.

As he sat beside his friend, Cyryl thought of the light that he had seen from the lighthouse tower shifting down towards the turbulent sea. The lighthouse was haunted. Every fisherman knew it; heard stories of the old lighthouse keeper and the circumstances of death and eerie hauntings that surrounded this place. When it was in use, it seemed to project the wraithlike light of doom. It was one of many fisherman tales told and retold as one of the legends surrounding this area of coastal sea. Some said it had lost its' power to save those lost at sea. A part of the mourning and sorrow that filled this light tower once meant for salvation and hope. Cyryl had not believed the story. It might be filled with sadness but the tower had projected its' light all the same, and those at sea in need of direction had been able to follow its' beam of light. True salvation was outside of any earthly light and found within the soul of a man. He was there on land, alive and proof of it.

It had been a week after that fortunate day on the sea that Cyryl had been offered the office work after making an inquiry as to the possibility of it. To his surprise, a position was offered to him. He had thought favorably about working in a mill or in place of business on land. He had thought of owning a piece of land and becoming a farmer. They were ordinary dreams of any man. He decided that the sea had made him cut off from life on land. He wanted a new beginning.

As a fisherman, Cyryl had assessed the varying weather, the way the sky looked on each day, from sunny to overcast and gray, or how the surface of the sea was flat and silent or rising and falling with much greater movement. Its' color changed too, like the sky and on certain days, sea and skies seemed to be the same in color and texture. Working on land had changed his view of the weather and the sky. The land and sky seemed less important as a setting. The manmade structures of the city more obvious. He had never felt so established in his daily living. His work separate from the physical elements of sea tides and shifting weather.

Being a fisherman was exhausting work; different from a sailor's life, lived far-off from land. A fisherman was more attached to the land

and the usual laws, rules and routine followed by the general society of a coastal town and that region.

When you were a sailor, the ship you lived on had its' own set of rules and interpretation of democracy, as they called it. There could be a lawlessness on these ships. Sailors became victims of it; countless deaths of men at sea for some reason or another, and often under mysterious or unexplained circumstances.

Sailors were outcasts of proper society. They were outside of what was considered clean and decent. The profession drew undesirables of all kinds and foreigners not to be trusted.

Fishing along the Eastern coast had become more difficult. The commercial fishing industry was changing. Hand lining for fish was no longer used since a hand liner had only one to four hooks. Fishermen in Massachusetts now used a technology called long lining, and a man could set 400 hooks on a line. Seine nets, had been hand made since the colonial days, but now they were machine made and were much larger and used with more frequency. These machine nets could catch whole schools of fish, such as mackerel, menhaden and herring. Yet, because the fish in shallow waters were growing scarce from decades of overfishing, the fishermen would have to venture farther out in their boats to make a good day's catch. The New England commercial fishing industry had recognized the problem and looked to the government for help; a restocking of fish in the ocean was needed.

While a fisherman, Cyryl had seen a Vincent Van Gogh (b.1853-d.1890) sun once, although he knew nothing of this foreign artist, Van Gogh. It was like a ball of sun-fire bursting, radiating above the horizon and then, the sea waves below it rising. He had told no one of his vision; that day fading to dusk like all other days, except for that vision of his, which he carried to his exhausted sleep. Then, the following day he had risen to another sea-soaked morning. He wondered what it had meant; this image of a beaming sun low in sky above turbulent sea waves. Certainly, it represented something important. It was a sign of a spiritual nature and a premonition of his future.

What did Cyryl look like? He was the most handsome man you could imagine and with a profile like that of a Greek statue. Yet, he wasn't a statue after all, but a flesh and blood Greek man. His brown eyes and dark curled hair could only have originated from that ancient culture and countryside. He was well-built and of an average height. To tell him he was short would have aroused his quick temper. He carried himself in a careful, masculine way that reflected his thoughtful and quiet intelligence. No one could help falling in love with him, if only for a moment as he paid for a purchase or stopped to look at something that he took notice to in a shop window. He could be elusive and introverted. Yet, there was something expressive in his face and manners that gave away his thoughts and moods. But this was not unpleasant to those around him. It made him even more attractive and easily definable. It is what impressed those that had hired him for work and with their more personal anecdotes. He was passionate in love and in his feeling about life in general.

Being deprived and without food had altered him. He had only gone hungry once; a period of two days before he was to receive his first pay as a fisherman. How could a fisherman go hungry? Wouldn't there be an abundance of fish? He was warned not to fish along the docks. He had eaten the salted cod pieces he had been given to eat, a charity from his employer. He had no money, no coins. It was so, and Cyryl went hungry and spent those two days in his room thinking about his next meal of chowder and a piece of bread. He didn't have the courage to ask for a credit at the local fisherman's restaurant. He doubted they would extend it, as he was a stranger in town and he knew of no one at that point in his life in Boston, who was more than an acquaintance. His hunger was mild in comparison to the hunger of others. He knew this as he had heard stories of real hunger from sailors and families who had endured severe poverty as new immigrants. It was still a terrible thing he thought, now being more familiar with it. An inhuman feeling and it was pitiless in its' result. To lack basic nourishment was a sin not just of the singular and private kind, but on all mankind, that might have a hand in such a result. Hunger was deprivation of the soul and spirit as well as the physical being. His stomach ached. The candle in his room grew smaller and smaller. It was the diminishing of hope. He too grew small on his cot, curled up in a fetal position and fully clothed. There was a lesson in the experience of it. Of going without sustenance or means. It would make him bolder in the pursuit of an opportunity and in providing for himself.

As he lay on his bed thinking, he remembered as an adolescent, once seeing a woman on the street in the city of New York. Adequately dressed and pleasant looking. She had taken notice of him. She looked like no one, but all women to him; a visual compilation of something female in form and a complete mystery. He had always been close to his mother. Yet, it seemed he didn't know women at all and being a very young man, it didn't bother him much at the time. But they remained a mystery to him even as he grew older, and although he found them beautiful and was even in awe of them at times, he knew that he would always be vague about them and he wasn't sure why.

Cyryl and his fisherman friend Stephen Blome had frequented the sailor and fisherman's regular haunt, Tally's Bar. Cyryl had tried to drink like the others. But the truth was he wasn't a drinker, not a real drinker, nor was his friend Stephen. He did not have to drink to forget or to be a man. He was a sensitive man and yet, he was strong in spirit and unwavering in his routine.

With Stephen, Cyryl had a bond of friendship that brought him closer to himself. In search of what he felt as a man and found of value in life. Stephen was someone in which he could share ideas and feelings. The two seemed to have a similar view on what was important in life and what was not. As a fisherman, that was what had elevated his existence, in a town that found sailors and fisherman of less status socially. Those meant to be kept in their position of labor and in the company of individuals of the same sort. Cyryl was always wishing to learn and he seemed to have the expectation of more in life. Stephen too, was smart and strong in spirit. He was logical and forthright in his thoughts and actions.

At Tally's Bar, sailors and fishermen would gather on a gray afternoon or on a dark night. The crowd was ugly or sometimes beautiful if you could make out the view through a haze of cigarette and cigar smoke. It was old and sad and failing in spirit, or fresh and newly tattooed. It was a crowd of liars in tattered clothes and yet some were in

21

their sailor's best and with the appearance of the good son of a Christian mother or father. It was a push and a pose as elegant as anything you might see on the most proper avenue of Victorian Boston. It was heartbreak and it was salvation, damnation and the endless search. Stephen and Cyryl, like all good friends watched out for each other in this place of alcohol consumption and consequential conversation.

"I remember the fish being plentiful just off shore," said an old fisherman with gray hair, to another man of a much younger age who had the looks of an Irishman.

"There's John over there ordering a beer!" said a young man who wore the uniform of a sailor. "Hello John," said the sailor, waving to a brown-haired man at the bar, in the same sailor uniform but added to; this being a jacket of a worn-looking suede.

Most of this conversation was lost in the general atmosphere of noise and in that form, it became private, but not as private as your own thoughts that contemplated the dinginess of the place and the reason for your being there. It was a gathering place on the edge of proper society and yet, here in this part of town, it was the center of it.

Stephen Blome for a time, had also been a sailor like Cyryl. In his twenties, he was blond-haired, slightly taller and larger in physical size than Cyryl and a good-looking man. He had been schooled at a young age in Boston and his spoken English was very good. He too was the son of immigrants, Dutch people. His father had died when he was young and his mother still resided in Boston. The two men looked magnificent together. One man was a Nordic blond and the other man, a dark Greek. They knew this and yet they never seemed outwardly conscious of it. They had been fated to meet, to become good friends and they enjoyed each other's company. They often spent their evenings together. But usually it was an early evening for them, as they were often tired from their day's work and knew that they had to rise just as early the following morning. Still, they found time to eat, drink a little and find the human pleasures that most sailors and fishermen seek on land.

"Let's go have a good dinner. Somewhere that serves meatloaf, brown beans, vegetables and cider cake," said Stephen.

"Cider cake!" said Cyryl.

Off they would go for a dinner and a walk about town. The two young men would walk the streets of Boston and comment on the many establishments and what they offered for sale. They might end up at Tally's Bar, but usually not as they preferred the peace and quiet of their rooms to this smoky place that was all about a tale of some sort that grew with the amount of liquor the storyteller had consumed. They had created for each other a kind of social regularity, despite both being single and tied to the sea.

It was another hard day's work for fisherman, Stephen Blome. He along with several other fishermen, had gone far out in a fishing vessel, into the coastal sea waters in search of a "good day's catch." Their machine-made nets were thrown out into rougher waters that day and the sun made bright, intermittent appearances in the sky, between long periods of it hidden behind large gray clouds. Cyryl was not with them.

For the same ground fishing company that he had fished for, Cyryl now worked in the capacity of a clerk in their offices and docks. He had done everything from cleaning the offices and warehouse, overseeing the fisherman docks, painting or varnishing boats, ordering and unloading supplies and running errands of all sorts. He was asked to do things he did not think he could do, but he would make the effort. He was careful and neat. He was consistent in everything he did and above all he could be trusted. He was not ordinary, but smart and reliable. If anything held him back, it was his inability to read and write properly.

"Cyryl, have you finished delivering the postal mail to the offices?" asked Mr. O'Malley, the office supervisor.

"Yes, sir, and I wrote the expenses into the ledger as you requested. I copied the numbers exactly as they were on each note," said Cyryl.

"Ok, you need to go and pick up some supplies downstairs in the main lobby. You will have to see that the new fishing nets are taken to the storage room. This afternoon we will head over to the docks and give out some of these," said Mr. O'Malley. "But first, I wish you to pick up some fishing tackle at Appleton & Litchfield. They are at 304 Washington Street. You will bring them a check which I will give to you before you leave." Cyryl had often delivered checks by hand, as the fishing company never used credit.

He could not read well, but well enough to understand most of what had been written for him as instructions from his supervisor, Mr. O'Malley. In one of the fishing company offices and on a desk, he had seen a copy of *Wide Awake, An Illustrated Magazine*, published by a Mr. D. Lothrop. It was a magazine of stories and illustrations for youth and family. O'Malley had noticed his curiosity.

"Education is good thing," said Mr. O'Malley. "On your day off, you should visit Harvard Yard, and look about the central area of Boston."

As was suggested to him, he made a discovery of the larger city of Boston, something he had not done at a younger age in New York City where he had grown up.

In this year, Boston was a city of many things; history, commerce, a sea port and a place of great learning. There was Ann Street, Beacon Street, Copley Square, Pemberton Square, Temple Street and Tremont Street. Streets and Squares with hotels, churches, schools, bakeries, theaters, an Opera House on Dudley Street, hardware stores, book stores, photogravure and photographic companies. There were theatrical costume companies, paper hangers and interior decorators, newspaper companies; an art museum and art galleries. There was even a place at Temple Place that sold ostrich feathers dyed in a variety of shades. These, places of society and commerce, he had seen on his walks in town. And as suggested to him, he had gone to see Harvard Yard in Cambridge, Massachusetts with his friend, Stephen Blome. They had admired the fine houses near the college. At first Stephen had balked at the idea but then he gave in at Cyryl's insistence.

"It will be good to get away from this part of town with its' smell of fish and sea water," said Cyryl. Stephen had admitted that even though he had grown up in Boston, much of it he had never seen.

At Harvard College, Cyryl remembered one building that they had been allowed to enter, but he could not remember what it housed. Inside, the stain glass in the windows from inside had glowed, as if revealing a secret of knowledge, waiting to be discovered. That was his most vivid memory of the day and the fact that he had shared it with Stephen. Walking the neighborhood, they had passed a book store that sold stationary goods.

24

"Let's buy postcards," said Stephen. It was unlike him to suggest such a thing, as it was usually Cyryl that wished to enter a store, to look around. Stephen would always look uninterested by this request to idle in a store filled with merchandise. The souvenir of their day was a small map of Boston and Cambridge, Massachusetts printed on a piece of heavy stock paper. It showed the Boston docks and surrounding area of Boston with its many neighborhoods. It even showed the area, where Stephen Blome had grown up as a child and where his mother still resided.

"Here is where I grew up," said Stephen. He pointed out his neighborhood to Cyryl. Seeing it on a map made it a place documented and important. The center of the world for any child and adult remembering.

They sat at the bar and had a glass of brown beer at a restaurant. They admired the neat interior and cleanliness of the place and the fine display of liquor behind the bar. The two men savored the taste of the brown beer.

"It is good beer," said Cyryl.

"Yes, a fine beer. I have never tasted such a good beer," said Stephen. "…It would be nice to be rich."

"Yes, and to have a fine house such as the ones we have seen today," said Cyryl. They sat for a moment without speaking, and then Cyryl had this thought.

"At times, my life seems not what I had thought it might be."

"What is it you want?" asked Stephen.

"I hope for a good life," said Cyryl.

"I don't think about my life as much as you, I guess. I take things as they come. What's the use of fretting over things?" asked Stephen.

"I think you are right," said Cyryl, nodding his head in agreement.

The idea of a better profession or attending a college to earn a degree did not enter their conversation, perhaps seeming outside of their social class and economic reach. It was good to be away from the rough edge of town where they resided. They took a horse-drawn street car across West End Bridge from Harvard Square into Boston and then walked the rest of the way. In the area where they lived, near the Boston docks, the streets were muddy. The buildings looked weather-worn and

25

were covered in dust. A horse and cart rumbled past them, with a load of lumber. The early evening sky had turned gold above the horizon. At least for a day, they had been Boston gentlemen.

Cyryl looked at of his new suit of clothes hanging nicely on a hanger in his room. With it on, he had looked at himself in the store's full-length mirror. How beautiful he looked in it. He looked Greek American. His hair thick and his eyes were dark. He was a proud man for this and for other reasons.

During that same month of June, Cyryl had visited the Boston Museum of Fine Arts, housed in a Gothic Revival building built of architectural terra cotta. The Boston Museum was a place Cyryl had seen pictured and written up in a Boston newspaper after he had found work as a fisherman in that city. It was something he put his mind to doing; going to this great museum to see American art. His friend, Stephen Blome had no interest in going to this museum with its' art and artifacts. He thought art a pastime for the wealthy or the artistic soul who was most often unappreciated and unpaid. Cyryl had gone by himself.

"One ticket please," said Cyryl, to the woman behind the desk.

"Could you direct me to the paintings?" asked Cyryl. "I would like to see paintings of American land."

"There are paintings in the gallery to your left, said the woman, directing Cyryl to a room that held American art portraits, landscapes and still life.

In other galleries of the museum there were classical busts in marble, paintings, collections of old coins and amazing natural artifacts. There were many examples of Greek vases and the oil-painted portraits of fine women and gentlemen. Centuries-old depictions of the blessed Madonna and child and landscape paintings of scenic places in Europe and America. Cyryl liked the landscape paintings of America best. Leaving there, he returned to his boarding house where he lived. His was a thrifty outing but an important one for him. He had experienced culture and he wrote home to his papa about it on a postcard with an image of the museum on Copley Square where he had visited. These were the things that made him different, a curiosity for life and learning. It was what would eventually make him dissatisfied with his life as a fisherman.

26

He had made a living from the sea and it seemed to bring him a certain calm, but he had grown dissatisfied with the limits of his existence. Most people lived their lives on land. Why he had never realized his discontent he could not quite fully understand. It was what he felt he must do; follow his father in this type of work. Be the good son and follow family tradition. But after a few years he realized that he was miserable and lonely as a fisherman. He was meant to work on land in an office, mill, a factory or on a farm.

If Cyryl had a flaw it would be that he was too proud a man. He saw his pursuit of employment in an office as an act of self-improvement. As a way of elevating his social class. His only work experience in an office had been as a clerk. His ability to read and write was limited. Yet, he did not think to pursue more aggressively the common labor jobs that might have been available to him in Boston. It would have been a setback for him. And so, it was a clerk position that he sought.

It was another day in October, one week after having been let go at the fishing company offices, that he decided to travel west. Anywhere away from the sea and the smell of salt air. It was already turning cold along the New England coast and he felt he had waited too long to leave. He had talked about leaving Boston to look for work elsewhere with his friend, Stephen Blome. Stephen had thought it a foolish notion. Cyryl's talk of leaving town angered him.

"You are just being stubborn," said Stephen. "If they have offered you work as a fisherman; then take it. It will be winter soon. What will you do then?" asked Stephen.

Cyryl needed to find work before winter. He *had* to find work. It was true that there were many mills and factories in the area. However, many people he met when he submitted his work application seemed suspicious of him. He was polite and assertive and yet, he was a foreigner still, it seemed; an out-of-work fisherman. His poor reading and writing ability did not help his prospects of finding another clerk position.

What Cyryl Megalos didn't see was that he was a remarkable man, of physical beauty and understanding of the human condition. Even without a proper education, he seemed superior to others around him. When he did converse with people, he did so with great honesty and

27

perception. One could see how he could easily be resented in a coarse, lower middle-class environment of brutal hard work and modest reward.

Cyryl had always shown curiosity in learning and he knew he was must be smart, as he had been told this by others.

"You have great potential, Cyryl!" his teachers at the New York City school had said. He looked the word up in a word dictionary and it made him frustrated. Potential was a sign of something you might be in the future. When he had been forced to leave school at the age of twelve to help support his family, he had been secretly heartbroken about it. His father had seen it in his eyes and his mother, who always had coddled him in ways, seemed without feeling in this manner. Too much education made one aloof and lazy. He was of a worker class. His hands and mind were made for manual labor. Too many books were a waste of time. He reminisced from time to time about his growing up on the Lower East Side of New York City. Mostly, he remembered the noise and the crowds of people. His idea of it was accurate in that it was a place of diverse humanity. The ordinary routine of countless lives cramped into one tiny place; hurried to some individual destination that defined them as poor, immigrant, male or female, adult or a child; of ill health or well. With a pace slow or fast, they moved toward that destination in hope of survival and something better.

Cyryl lay in his bed that afternoon, listening to the rain, half asleep and he thought of his early childhood growing up in New York. He had thought he had heard rain the night before, wishing for it, but it had only been the sound of a strong wind. Now the sound of real rain brought him back to an unidentified day of cloudy skies threatening the same precipitation. His thoughts had again gone back to his childhood on the Lower East Side of New York City. The sounds and images of the place returned to him, at first far away and distant and then with more detail, color and tonality. There was a woman wearing a navy-blue skirt and a white blouse clutching the hand of her daughter as they made their way down a crowded street.

"Don't walk away from me!" the mother had said to the small girl. Survival was foremost in this immigrant place of young deaths and great human toil.

There were men in different hats and caps, some men or boys without one and Cyryl wondered why? A boy or a man should always wear a hat or a cap he thought. Outside of storefronts merchandise filled wooden bins and pushcarts offered food or other items like pots and pans. His mother would say how wide his shoulders were and what nice thick dark hair he had. What a handsome man he would make someday.

"Cyryl, your shoulders are wide and strong looking! You have hair like my father, dark, thick and curly. You will be a handsome Greek man someday," said Mrs. Megalos to her son. Cyryl did not know how to respond to his mother's compliments except to smile. He always remembered though, that he had wide and strong shoulders and it helped him to have confidence on days when he seemed to have very little.

Nature seemed pushed to the side in the crowded city streets of New York. Only a sooty memory of it remained in patches of blue sky and narrow areas of grass around the structures of commerce and habitation. The rural memories of these residents were vivid; Irish hills of green, Greek fields of olive trees or a German scene of forests. America offered rural scenes just as beautiful and some of these immigrants would move on to see them. Yet, many others would remain in New York City or Boston or another American city and accept their new surroundings of brick and wood structures, one after another crowded with humanity. Here in the city was survival and community for the immigrant and it seemed more important than a scenic rural view. There was always the hope of a vacation or a seaside visit. Hope was what kept these people alive. The same hope that had carried them across the Atlantic Ocean, dark blue, shimmering and endless.

Cyryl had heard many stories about Greece from his parents. And as a young man, Cyryl had thought about returning to Greece, to where most of his relatives still lived. But the cost and the distance discouraged any real contemplation of a trip to this South-Eastern European country. His image of this place was derived from his parent's recollected memories and the few photographs he had seen of the landscape and towns of Greece. His limited knowledge of the world and its' wonders was mind images of Asian foreigners, the great pyramids of Egypt (these he had seen in a photograph as well), the metropolis of London and Paris and the center of the Catholic religion, Rome, Italy. There were the

South Seas with savages, sand beaches and palm trees and the sparkling blue Mediterranean Sea that was a source of living for many Greek men. There was vast and exotic India and the North and South Poles covered in snow. But here he was in America, the land of promise. He was Greek and American. He had been born here, in New York City and unlike his parents, America was his homeland.

He was no longer in New York City but living in the state of Massachusetts and in the town of Boston. This coastal town of brick buildings and stone streets looked damp and gray that fall morning. The long-tangled blades of grass in the Boston graveyard were wet from the previous night's rainfall. The clopping sound of horse hooves pulling a carriage could be heard on a side street as part of the day's activity commenced. The horse and carriage still unseen, the noise seemed outside of this world. As if produced by some other force masking itself in a familiar human tone of action. It appeared with its driver, a stern, gray-haired man in a thick wool coat, setting out that morning as he always did to some destination of employment.

He had gained a sense of Boston as a town of American Colonial history. In comparison to New York City, that seemed more influenced by its' large immigrant populations of many cultural origins. Both were seaports and centers of trade and industry. Each metropolis with its' own integration of architectural styles; Georgian, Federal, Greek Revival, Italianate, Second Empire and Romanesque. New York City seemed to be made of its' activity. Yet, what narration Boston held was within its' structured elements. Truly American in its' appearance. American being Colonial, courageous, intellectualized and born of the grit of ordinary citizenry who had hoped and toiled towards something better and within the new rules of democracy and the ideals of a unified republic. Cyryl was a part of that history now, like the stone cherub that had been carved onto a façade, as a record of a style and an era. It was this very stone element that he stared up at, as he contemplated his next interview for employment.

He had decided to give it one more day. But upon returning home that evening with no prospects, he was resolute in his decision to leave Boston and to look for work elsewhere and inland; otherwise face work as a fisherman.

On his way towards home, Cyryl had caught a glimpse of the sea. It opposed him. It was there in the sound and surface of the sea. As if a resonate from a previous time of old.

He knew he would not return to work as a fisherman but the way forward seemed uncertain. There was his friend Stephen. He would have to say goodbye to him if he left Boston. He wished for Stephen to go with him on his journey to look for work, but the prospect seemed unlikely. He would leave him then, to his life as a fisherman. Yet, something inside of Cyryl knew this was not to be either. They had become friends out of loneliness, partly due to the life of a fisherman and what they had in common as former sailors and being men, seemingly outside of the normal mode of living.

Before leaving Boston, Cyryl said goodbye to his fisherman friends. Most of them lived at the same place, a boarding house that rented rooms. His greatest friend being Stephen, the blond-haired American Dutchman.

Cyryl went to say goodbye to Stephen, who seemed cross at first when he was told of Cyryl leaving to find work on land. Stephen could be too quick-tempered and he argued with Cyryl against such a decision. Stephen had somewhat known of his plan, but he had not fully realized that Cyryl was set on it. At this moment, Stephen was sad and overcome with affection for his departing friend Cyryl.

"I did not think you would really leave here and leave me, your best friend. I will miss you. Now all that is left for me is the sea," said Stephen.

"Come with me then," said Cyryl.

"No, I will become a sailor again," said Stephen.

"You love the sea," said Cyryl.

"Yes, a part of me does and always will," said Stephen.

"A sailor always then," said Cyryl. He thought Stephen might have gone along with him, if he had asked.

"Yes, a sailor at heart, I suppose. You will make a good farmer. I know you will. veel geluk (good luck) Cyryl, veel geluk!" said Stephen, in Dutch. His voice wishing him good luck had a sound of misery. It was something he had wished Cyryl in the morning before his day of fishing.

"Good bye, Stephen," said Cyryl. "I will write to you and send you postcards."

They embraced each other for a moment and then Cyryl went on his way, not looking back this time. They had always had a practice of looking back and waving to each other as a sign of loyalty and friendship. The rest of them had told him he should not look back. The life of a fisherman or a sailor was not what it should be. You were a lost man if you were a sailor with never a real place to call home. Sea was your home and no home it was at all, but a dark reflection of what might be in a man's life. Being a fisherman meant living on land usually, but many of these fishermen-sailors would then return to the sea on ships departing for long voyages. They could not seem to stay on land for long, before the sea would beckon them to another far-away foreign shore and a dark-blue or green ocean. The thought had bothered Cyryl. He imagined himself lost at sea and returning as an old broken man. Just like the old sailors who sat drinking whiskey at Tally's Bar. These were pitiful old men with sad eyes and thick forearms that showed once manly tattoos shriveled with the age on their sun-burnt skin. Anchors and crudely drawn sailing ships were the most popular of these ink drawings. These old sailors seemed to dream their own dreams and the floating clouds of those dreams were found in the liquid of a whiskey glass or a fading beer. He felt he must leave.

Cyryl felt a bit foolish for he already felt lonely and fearful. Along with his father and older sister that he wrote to in New York City, these men were the only family that he had known; his mother and the aunts and uncles he remembered resting in heaven and looking down on him. He didn't question his decision but he hoped he had good luck in finding new work and a place for himself. He would miss his friend Stephen more than the others.

He was on the street now heading back towards his boarding-house room. He heard a voice calling out his name. It was Stephen. At the last minute, Stephen Blome had decided to join Cyryl in his search for work on land. He'd had a change of heart about it all. The two would be more successful if they went off together; to look out for each other.

"It would be foolish of you to go off on your own. I'll go with you," said Stephen. You know how you are, dreaming of things you cannot own or be," said Stephen. "You will be broke in a week and with no place to live!"

Cyryl was immensely happy at his decision but he had only slightly smiled at his announcement. When Stephen had mentioned returning to a sailor's life, he had wanted to express his disapproval. He was glad he had kept silent. It was Stephen's own decision and he couldn't blame Cyryl if it all turned out badly. Yet, Cyryl couldn't imagine that it would. He simply had too much youthful hope and expectation, in life and in his own sound capability. He postponed his trip for a few days so that Stephen Blome could get his affairs in order. He was at times, concerned that Stephen might have a change of heart but he followed through with it all and Stephen said goodbye to his mother, who seemed very surprised by her son's sudden decision. If he were to leave this town for someplace unknown, then it was best he go with his good friend, Cyryl.

As with most things, Cyryl Megalos had approached his new beginning with an air of seriousness. It was a journey of destiny and personal progress, like the one his parents had taken when immigrants from Greece. Like all journeys it had required a preparation and a bit of drama. Cyryl had bought a suitcase at a second-hand shop on Nation Street. It was covered in worn brown leather and trimmed at the corners with metal. It had looked very sturdy to him, although he felt he had spent too much for it, even after bargaining with the shop owner. Stephen only had brought along his canvas duffle bag.

It was decided that they would first take a train West and a distance from the coast to an area of farms and factories. After the purchasing of tickets, they boarded the train and settled themselves in their seats.

The view of the American landscape from the train window was varied green and in colors of yellow and brown. When seen, the newly built fabrications of man now made nature seem more of a mystery. The structures built outside of the larger cities, an indication of the industry within them. In the small towns the train passed through, the activity of people was connected to the season. Evidence of this was seen in the wagons that brought produce to town or the farmer and his wife buying supplies for winter. It seemed that the American spirit had survived the terrible effects of the Civil War. It was hope and faith that had kept them unwavering and prosperous. Yet, within the landscape, the country's Civil War had been chronicled and the branches of trees, advanced and crossed, held remembrance of those lost in that mortal conflict.

In the thriving Eastern states, there were many good people and some that were ignorant or even criminal. Political cartoons, caustic and humorous in New England publications or posted on a whitewashed wall, hoped to sway the opinions of the voting public.

With a consideration of the money they would expend on their tickets, the two men had decided to take the passenger train West all the way to the town of New Lebanon, New York.

The conductor made the announcement of the New Lebanon, New York stop. Then they found themselves on the train station platform.

The train had altered this New York State town as much as any town now connected to this mode of travel and shipping. The approach of it could be seen from a distance. Its' locomotive's dense, billowing smoke rising into the blue sky. The citizens of the town would wait for its' arrival; listen for its' mechanical noise and whistle.

In New Lebanon, New York, there was a kind of freedom expressed in the movement of the town's people; polite or brash. The conversations loud or soft and meant to distract or persuade. The normal activity of any American town. Within it was the spirit of the American revolution and the relief that a divided union had been made whole again.

After eating lunch, the two men inquired about factory or mill work and were told there was little to none, for unskilled fishermen. They found a place for the night and on the second day, their inquiries for work led them to a man traveling West that told them there might be work on a farm along the way. And so, being discouraged and with nothing to lose, they rode with the man in search of rural work.

Now they traveled more slowly across the New York countryside. Other roads they crossed led to small towns thriving and farms with fields of crops and grazing land. In between these places were the unscathed valleys and hills of wild woods, grassy flat-lands and streams. In the distance seen, was the train following its' track. Its' smoke and noise seemed an intrusion to the natural setting around it, and yet it was a product of it.

The surrounding tree-covered hills were a darker green than the valley land, covered in grass below. The horse and buggy now made its way through the Appalachian valley area of Mount Lebanon, New York. Cyryl looked out at the horizon. A sliver of white light was visible, radiating above the tree tops along the horizon. The sky was a pale blue and it was a place that looked fertile and that had a peacefulness about it.

"I think this would be a good place to start a farm," said Cyryl. Stephen at first said nothing but looked out at the sky in the distance.

"It looks like good land," said Stephen.

"Well, I've an idea for you, now that you mention it. I had thought of it before," said the driver.

"The Shakers live in this area. Ever hear of them?" asked the driver. "They are a religious group of individuals that are well-respected around here. They own a big piece of fine land here, with many fine buildings. They're farmers among other things, and they are always looking to hire workmen. You might just get out right here as it is near their community and ask for a job as workmen. I'll bet you'd be offered something. At the very least, they will put you up for a night. They need good strong men to do their regular labor. They are always looking to hire sober and reliable men. Tell them that you are hard workers," said the driver.

"It's worth a try. It sounds like they might have some work for us. That sky is foretelling of colder weather. I have worked in the fields and on a farm before," said Stephen.

Cyryl and Stephen knew nothing of these Shakers and so the buggy driver told him what he knew of their spiritual community and their success at many things including irrigation of the valley for crops, and the many industries they had as part of their community profiting.

"They make furniture and sell produce. They make the best liquor you ever tasted! They are severe people and dress all the same but they are kind folks, he said. I know the workmen live a distance from the main buildings of the community. You might get a bed tonight and start your farming tomorrow," said the driver with encouragement.

Cyryl felt an exhilaration in the chance of it. He thought the white light above the horizon to be a good sign; an omen. Stephen thought it worth a try. The man's logic and words gave them the mettle to walk the distance from the road to the area where they might find work on the

Shaker farm. They said their goodbye to the driver after paying a modest sum for their transportation. They watched him as he followed the road in his buggy down a hill and disappear.

Cyryl and Stephen were now somewhat apprehensive. They had no certain place to spend the night and they had no idea what these Shaker people might do for them; two out-of-work, sailor-fisherman. Had they been too quick in their decision to give up their traveling companion and the safety of the horse and buggy? Cyryl and Stephen would soon find out.

The side road to the Shaker village cut through hills thick with birch, elm and oak trees. Outcrops of granite were a feature of the mostly flat and fertile land. They approached a narrow river that seemed to flow from the hills in the distance. The sunlight on the river made it look green. It was the sunlight filtered through the leaves of an elm tree that shaded its' bank. The tree leaves casting patterns of shadow onto the grass. The shadowed grass rendered as blue. The rich brown earth of the field land was just visible and moths, wasps and bugs of every sort flittered about above the weeds, wild-flowers and the grass that covered it. Walking onward, they saw a few buildings about a quarter mile ahead and assumed these were part of the Shaker community. They were in fact Shaker storehouses for goods. But also, not far, was the place where the hired men lived that worked for the Shakers. The driver had been right and he had seemed to know just where to let Cyryl and Stephen off along the road, for them to find their way. Life could be like that and or it could be a lost journey. It was another sign of good luck Cyryl thought; this accurate direction and the sunlight along the horizon.

II

The End Of Fall

New Lebanon, New York Shaker Community, 1887

It was a Monday morning and the activity of daily labor had commenced at the Mount Lebanon, New York Shaker Community. It appeared as if all parts of this scenic place were filled with a labor or industry of some kind. In the planted fields and lower hills, in all useful buildings and in the family dwelling houses, all hands had begun their assigned tasks. Shaker sisters in the kitchen of the North Family house were preparing harvested fruits and vegetables for canning. The Shaker sisters had picked these vegetables from the garden and they had placed them into Shaker baskets. These would be trimmed and cleaned before being canned.

"Sisters, we have finished putting up the cucumbers and peaches. What are left are the carrots and green beans. There are plenty of glass jars and lids for these," said Shaker Sister Emily. Shaker Sister Emily was one of the Shaker sisters that would oversee the work of the kitchen sisters and the work in the Shaker gardens, a favorite place for her.

As with the cucumbers, the carrots and green beans would be preserved in spring water. The fruits had been steeped to form their own vinegar for preserving. The finished jars were put on shelves in the pantry where these were stored. Some of these would be sold for a profit. They had been sealed and labeled with the script letters of a Shaker sister's hand; neatly spaced legible letters that identified the vegetable or fruit within, such as *B l a c k –b e r r i e s* or *P e a c h e s*.

Shaker Brother Thomas and Shaker Brother Matthew were about to set out on a trip to sell Shaker goods in a nearby town.

Shaker Brother Matthew was now twenty-seven years of age. If ever a Shaker Brother had sex appeal, it was Shaker Brother Matthew. It was simply a part of his masculine character. Yet, it seemed to rest inside of him completely dormant. And too, the Shakers were a celibate religious community.

Shaker Brother Matthew was of Irish descent, tall at six feet in height and he was of a lean, strong build. His complexion was fair and his hair was dark, reddish-brown and shortly-cropped. His face was pleasant and handsome and it often held a look of contemplation. He frequently found himself deep in thought. He had more conservative views that even some of the elder Shakers. He strongly believed in equality for men and women. He was always open to new ideas in the pursuit of economic advancement for the community. No newly invented machine or tool when heard of, was too modern to be considered for use. But when it came to spiritual devotion, he was most concerned in maintaining the established laws and traditions of the early Shaker believers. He often quoted Mother Ann Lee or a Shaker that had been admired for their spiritual writings and devout Shaker faith. For such a young man, he had a very old soul. He would have made a great father and in a sense, he had become one. He was greatly concerned for the youngest Shaker members; the children.

Shaker Brother Thomas was in his late fifties. He was of an average height, a stout man and his remaining hair around the crown of his head was now as white as snow. He had ruddy cheeks and his face, even in Shaker prayer meetings looked serene and smiling. Yet, when displeased, his pleasant face could change to look sour and dissatisfied. The Shaker sisters compared his disposition to the many herbs they grew; sweet to bitter.

The horses reared and stepped back pushing the carriage a distance. The Shaker brothers calmed the horses as more goods were put into the back of the carriage for a trip to a nearby town. It was starting to rain, a sprinkling from a sky with gray clouds that was still partially sunny. Would it rain harder? It didn't seem likely by the looks of it, but a wool blanket was brought to the carriage to cover its contents if such weather came upon them. Vegetables and herbs, seeds and other items for the general store had now been loaded onto the carriage. A set of ladder back chairs promised to a family in town was also now loaded onto the carriage along with the produce.

"Is that all of it?" asked Shaker Brother Thomas.

"I believe so, brother," said Shaker Brother Matthew.

"Well, let's be on our way," said Shaker Brother Thomas.

They traveled along the road into town. The rain had almost stopped and the sun shined brighter as a gray cloud moved away from it, exposing its brilliant light. In the distance, the varied green landscape of valley and hills looked luminous. A cool wind blew and the leaves of the big oak tree near one of the family houses dropped rain onto them as they passed by in the carriage with their goods. It would be a good day of profit and a pleasant trip through this New York State land.

Cyryl and Stephen now sat inside a basement office within the hirelings dwelling house at the Mount Lebanon Shaker Village. They were speaking to the farm deacon, a man named Harren, who oversaw the hired men's work at the Shaker Village. They had waited almost two hours and their initial eagerness had waned somewhat. An apprehension grew between them as they wondered of the possibility of being turned away without work or a place to stay. Cyryl now started to wonder if it had been foolish to travel without a specific destination. Something his father probably would not have done. Things were to be planned and thought about. A man didn't just take off for no reason at all. But he did have a reason. As good a reason as the land he had traveled by foot that day. That American land was the reason. His reason being his wish to farm or to work on land in some capacity and he thought of the landscape paintings he had seen at the museum in Boston that had inspired his journey from the coast. Stephen had joined him as he had hoped.

They finally were to have their interview with the farm deacon, who now sat behind his desk.

Harren, the Shaker farm deacon, was not of the Shaker faith himself, but he also had been hired by the Shaker Brothers and Sisters at Mount Lebanon, to assist with the management of their large land holdings and related community industries. He was a man in his thirties, good looking, meticulously clean and of above average height. He seemed well-educated and knowledgeable of the Shakers, farms and the managing of them.

"Hello, men. I was in a meeting with the Shaker brothers. Thank you for waiting. I assume you are here to apply for work," said Harren.

"We have traveled all the way from the city of Boston, Massachusetts," said Cyryl. We are looking for work. I've worked as a clerk in the offices, warehouse and docks of a well-respected fishing company, The Doverman Fishing Company. I have a written reference if you wish to see it. Cyryl handed the farm deacon his neatly folded letter of reference inside an envelope. I have also worked as a fisherman. The fishing company was sold this past summer, I lost my job or rather my work ended and so I have decided to seek other work farther West and more inland. You see, by knowing the kind of hard work I have known and helping to support my family when growing up in New York City, I am fit for most work. I want to be a farmer someday. I am strong and healthy and looking for a good place for myself. I was told you hire men here for work on the Shaker farm."

"I am experienced at farm work and as a fisherman, knowing hard work as well," said Stephen Blome.

"Well gentlemen, it's not just a farm here but a whole community. We only hire sober men; men that haven't seen any trouble with the law. You're not running from the law, are you?" asked the farm deacon.

"Oh, no!" said Cyryl. He had frowned at the thought.

"I am a Greek American citizen with no record of trouble or offensives. I am most sincere in finding work," said Cyryl.

"I have had no trouble of that kind either," said Stephen.

"You'd live here in the men's dwelling house and bunk with the other workmen in a room that isn't so private. We provide a pail shower or bath and three meals a day and your pay is paid out monthly. You must agree to stay a minimum of three to six months. You are paid for eight hours of work each day, Monday through Friday or Tuesday through Saturday. No man works a Sunday here. You say you are well and fit and sober men?" asked the farm deacon.

"Yes, I am well and sober and strong."

"I am too sir," said Stephen.

"Glad, to hear of it," said Harren.

40

"Well, Cyryl and Stephen, I think you have found yourself jobs. I do the hiring here but you will need to also meet one of the Shaker brothers. You two should clean yourselves up first. I'll show you where you will sleep. You can put your things on the shelf and in a drawer under your bed that we provide for you. No drinking of alcohol or stealing here or you are gone," said Harren.

"Yes sir. We wouldn't steal," said Cyryl, looking at his friend Stephen.

"Well, see that you don't," said Harren.

"The dinner meal is served at 6:00 pm and be on time. There's always plenty to eat from the Shaker gardens and the best bread you ever tasted. I always ask. Are you interested in becoming a Shaker?" asked the farm deacon.

Cyryl was afraid to say something that might sound negative or non-spiritual.

"Well, that is not likely but my mother taught me about Christ as our savior," said Cyryl.

Stephen was silent in response to the question.

"That is something then that you can discuss with a Shaker brother in due time. There's probably a lot you do not know about the Shaker faith," said Harren.

The farm deacon then showed Cyryl and Stephen their sleeping accommodations. Their beds were next to the bed of a man named Bill Patterson. Bill was a young man from Pennsylvania. He was put together solidly and his wide shoulders and large biceps strained against his cotton shirts. He was the kind of a man a woman would love passionately.

Bill introduced himself that day to Cyryl and Stephen. He was full of talk about himself, but then he grew curious about Cyryl and his background.

"You're a Greek fellow. You're the son of Greek Immigrants Harren told me," said Bill.

"How do you do? said Cyryl. "My name is Cyryl Megalos."

"Hello, I am Stephen Blome," said Stephen, offering a hand shake.

"I'm Bill Patterson. There's a lot of work to be done here, year-round, as there are fewer male Shaker members," said Bill. He had not

41

left like many of the hired workers had done, at the beginning of that previous summer, but had stayed on with the approval of Harren, the farm deacon.

That early evening and after a fine dinner, Cyryl and Stephen were spoken to by a Shaker brother.

"I am told that you two men were fishermen in the city of Boston. What qualifies you for farm labor?" asked the Shaker brother.

"I worked on farms while growing up in Massachusetts, gardening and weeding and such," said Stephen.

"Much of the work of a fisherman is done on land. We are good workers," said Cyryl.

"Well, I would guess this is a different sort of work, but you know hard work, and you are sober men, honest and steady men, then you are welcome here. The colder weather is coming. The harvest month of October is almost gone, yet there is much work to be done," said the Shaker brother.

Later, they rested in their beds before going to sleep. The long day's journey and the meal had made them very sleepy.

"See, I told you we would find work," said Cyryl.

"I think we were lucky to have found anything this late in the season," said Stephen.

They both admitted to feeling very lucky to have found a place to work and live. The cold weather of late fall would soon come and Cyryl and Stephen would recall their fortunate trip made from the port of Boston, Massachusetts prior to their arrival at Mount Lebanon, New York.

A breakfast for the hired workmen that following morning consisted of fried eggs and ham on Shaker made-bread with strawberry jam, a helping of butter and a strong cup of Shaker tea. Cyryl was first to work in the poultry house and Stephen was to help clean the wash house. Both men preferred to work outdoors but they never mentioned this to the farm deacon or Shaker brothers. The work was reasonable and the company of others not unpleasant or rough. The workmen talked and laughed amongst themselves. Many were Irishmen; one of them an Italian American and another, a black man who had gone North after the Civil War. They were beautiful men in their simple manner and dress

42

and if not educated, schooled in the basic rules of social friendliness and a sense of American pride. There were hired women as well. They were housed in another Shaker building. Women who had a special skill like weaving or tailoring. They wore worldly dress but of the plainest kind except for a hat or coat or a shawl that gave away their sense of style and taste for the fashions of the day.

There was a discussion of the Shaker harvest and the irrigation of the planted fields.

"The improved irrigation of the crop fields seems a success," said Shaker Brother Matthew.

"Yes, but I would advise that we make some more improvements to the system before cold weather sets in so that we are prepared for the spring planting," said another Shaker brother.

"We will get it done. I have spoken with the farm deacon and he will organize the workmen to do this," said Shaker Brother Matthew.

Cyryl and Stephen were to help with the water irrigation project. In fact, it was to be a good part of their work for the next two weeks. Many of the hired workmen had been put on this task. A vast irrigation system had been worked out by the Shaker brothers. Fresh spring water from the hills now flowed to the valley to irrigate the Shaker crops. Shaker Brother Matthew documented the work with his wood and brass field camera. The workmen walked towards the hills where they were to help dig irrigation trenches. These low green hills seemed an extension of the valley. Their color the same as the lower valley and sloping gently to a higher elevation.

It was a good, dry and sunny day for work. A morning breeze made it pleasant to be outdoors. Cyryl and Stephen were given tin cups to taste the stream water; fresh and pure it was, and used for drinking as well as irrigation.

It was mid-week now and Cyryl was tired from the previous day's work. His hands were calloused and his lower back ached. It would be another day of work on the irrigation system for the Shaker community. The sun was shining bright. Bill Patterson worked alongside him that day. It gave them a chance to talk and dream about the future.

"My dad has a small farm in Pennsylvania. I just up and left one day. I guess I am running away from things" said Bill.

"What was it that you ran away from?" asked Cyryl.

"Responsibilities I suppose," said Bill.

"What do you mean?" asked Cyryl.

"I didn't want to settle down just yet and marry and have kids. The country girls want you to marry them right off. I had gotten into trouble once or twice and staying would have meant more trouble. My dad and I were not getting along. It upset my mother and sisters that I left. I miss my younger brother. I write them twice a month. I'll go back. The Shakers pay good wages. Here I can save some money and then return to Pennsylvania and start out on my own," said Bill.

"I have the same plan," said Cyryl. "I want to earn and save up wages and then buy a small farm and some land."

Bill continued with his talk of home.

"There was one farm girl, the daughter of one of our neighbors. She would invite me over to her dad's farm and then giggle and bring me things to eat like apple pie or corn bread. She really liked to eat. I imagined us both in the same kitchen eating together, older and fat. So, you got tired of being a fisherman then?" asked Bill.

"I was tired of it. It was hard work. Also, the fish are disappearing from the coastal waters because of overfishing. No respectable man should work as a fisherman. I don't care what my father says. He was a fisherman in Greece when he was a young man. His father's father and his father before him; a family curse I call it. He then worked on the docks in New York City near South Street. My parents immigrated to America from Greece. My mother is now in heaven. My father is alive and I have one sister. You know, I would get sea sick? I never liked it much," said Cyryl.

"I guess not then. What kind of farming are you going to do?" asked Bill.

"Well, the most profitable and easiest kind I would think; cows for milking and chickens and land for grazing and crops. I guess I haven't thought about it that much," said Cyryl.

"You should raise some cattle and sell them. You can always make some money doing that. But you'll need seed money to start. You should try to find a place you can buy a little at a time. That's what my dad did but that was a long time ago, way back when land real cheap and unused.

A lot of Pennsylvania land is fertile for farming but a lot of it just good for lumber.

"The place I would like would have acres of flat land for crops. I would have a garden just like the Shakers have near the house. A barn and a shed and ...a chicken coop," said Cyryl.

Bill laughed when Cyryl said this. He didn't seem to know much about farming. The two continued to widen the ditch that would carry water from the surrounding hills.

"Do you know how this valley was made?" asked Bill.

"What do you mean?" asked Cyryl.

"I mean this valley were in. It was carved from big sheets of ice coming down from the North. Glaciers they call them."

"It was made by God. I am sure the Shakers wouldn't like hearing you talk that way," said Cyryl.

Bill laughed again.

"I am not talking about the creation of the earth. That was from an explosion in space. I mean much later," said Bill.

"God made all things. I learned that when I was a small boy. You don't believe in God?" asked Cyryl.

"I think there is a God. But I wish he paid notice more often. This whole area used to be a mountain range of rock but it was worn down from those sheets of ice and time. I mean centuries of time and erosion," said Bill.

"Where did you learn all this?" asked Cyryl.

"I learned it in school. Didn't you go to school?" asked Bill.

"Sure, I did, but for things like writing and reading. And learning math and I don't remember the rest; American History! I learned about George Washington and Thomas Jefferson. Good patriotic men like that," said Cyryl. He had grown emotional in his response as if defending his unshakable belief in America.

"Well, I think that Republican fellow from Ohio, James Garfield is going to be our next U.S. President, said Bill. "He's running against that Civil War General, Winfield Scott Hancock. He's also from Pennsylvania but I wouldn't vote for him. Too many young men died in that war. I want nothing to do with Civil War Generals," said Bill. "I remember it all from when I was just a boy."

Listening to Bill, Cyryl recognized that both he and Bill had avoided being soldiers in the Civil War because of their age. America was still very much frayed by the war. There had been so much heartbreak, death and conflict. A lot of bitterness remained between North and South, Republican and Democrat. President Lincoln's assassination remained as a shadow over the country.

In the evenings after dinner, the workmen shared tales of their relatives and the reasons why they were there in that rural New York county and circumstance. When they talked of women they kept it more private, laughing and telling stories of female conquests that avoided true love and the complications of a married union. They smoked tobacco, were rough in manners at times, and some drank in town once paid their wages and idle. But they knew to hold themselves as proper men and consistent in their work and propriety before the farm deacon and the Shakers.

It was another day of work. With Shaker-made shovels, Bill, Cyryl, Stephen and the others now struggled with the digging of earth under the afternoon sun. Cyryl had always worked hard but it had been on the sea. Now he was on land and working just as hard. It was a different kind of work. There was the ground beneath him and trees in the distance on the surrounding low hills. He had already grown to love this valley. It wasn't a dramatic landscape but one of rolling hills and valleys. You always felt close to the earth here. It was a place to farm and a place to plant things that grew. And grow they did. The irrigation system the Shakers had devised was as ingenious and innovative as their many other projects that involved the building of architecture and the production of goods to sell. Crops grew tall in the fields. The water along with the sun and good soil worked their miracle. The bounty of the lord was the result; vegetables and herbs and fruit and hay. It was picturesque to see and it made the village acreage impressive to the passing visitor. Cyryl had learned more about farming at this point than he realized. Someday he would apply what he had learned to his own farming. He now stopped and wiped his brow with a handkerchief he kept in the front pocket of his pants. It was hard work, but the day would end soon enough. He had done it. He was working on land. His papa would be proud of him. The sea seemed a great distance away.

Shaker sisters and Shaker Brother Matthew were standing near a family house and discussing the results of their labor.

"Brother Matthew, what is your opinion of our harvest from the fruit trees?" asked a Shaker sister. "There seemed an increase in the amount of peaches and apples this season."

"I would say that to be accurate and with apples still to be picked and gathered," said Brother Matthew. "An abundance of apples fallen from the trees."

"Yes, a daily count of these that a sister will gather," said a Shaker sister.

The sun was hidden behind a mountain and the lack of direct daylight had made things a darker hue; the landscape and its' trees. The cooler weather and wind told you it could only be autumn. The apples on the leaf covered ground in the orchard were waiting to be made into apple sauce and pie.

It was Shaker Elder Milo who knew much about the orchards and he had made many transcriptions on the cultivating of fruits. He was a very tall man and he was often able to reach the lower branches of the trees when picking or examining a specimen of produce in the Shaker orchards. He was just as knowledgeable of gardens and the right conditions for growth and bounty of vegetables and flowers. He used a cane fashioned from red oak. Its' natural bend suitable for gripping. Age had left him visibly older but not so much in his posture and stride. His physical stamina had remained intact. He had a steady gaze that seemed to go beyond the average visual surmise; precise in its' interpretation and weight of his surroundings. The physical setting of Mount Lebanon suited him and he loved its' beauty and mountainous land. No one could argue that he was not Appalachian in his acclimated state of being; showing great appreciation for the plenteousness of natural resources found there.

You wondered what the day might bring. With the sunlight dim and the land yet mostly dark. You faced it with hope as with all days. The Shakers giving thanks for it.

In the community, there were many different tasks connected to the range of industry that was the Shaker commerce at Mount Lebanon. In this fall season, as part of this work, large quantities of vegetables and

47

fruit were picked and brought indoors in metal pails and Shaker baskets. The yielding of produce continued for several days and after one day of work in the fields and gardens. Shaker brothers and sisters gathered to see the results in pails and wagons. To those gathered, Shaker Brother Milo said,

"We have a good land to provide food for us. Look at the harvest that we have made with the help of our Lord and Savior. We bless this bounty in your name Jesus our Lord, amen."

The sound of the word "amen" was repeated from the Shakers standing there in the late afternoon light. A light more gold than white and that washed one section of a family house. Its' light leaving an angle of shadow onto the side of the house and the grass-covered ground. It had been a good day of hard work made by many hands.

Fall in New York State had been a blaze of color but the orange-crimson and yellow leaves had fallen from the trees. Winter was coming. A chilly November air shook the bare branches of the trees and reflected their shadows onto the land surrounding the Mount Lebanon Shaker Village. Yes, Winter was coming and there were many tasks to accomplish; hands to work, hearts to God.

The day for the Mount Lebanon Shaker Village started early. The morning sun could illuminate the sky or never seemed to rise if hidden by gray clouds. This morning God had offered a mix of sunshine along the horizon and white-gray clouds in a pale-blue sky. It was a very cold morning for fall. A morning that made sounds echo louder as if to announce it. Like the scrap of a pail on the floor or a door latch being opened. God's earth had given them a bounty of food. They would thank him for it; that day and many others. Steady and hard work had brought prosperity and the Shakers never ceased to be thankful and amazed by this very fact. For the Lord's goodness was boundless and they had been brought to a fruitful land, pure clean water, wood for timber, wool for clothing and comfort, vegetables and fruit for canning and herbs for flavoring and medicines. With stern and steady work and this abundance bestowed upon them, they could create a place of living, of utopia for him here on earth where the separation of good and evil had begun in preparation for the lord's return to earth. All things were possible with the lord.

As for the Shaker structures built on this land, there was a perfect symmetry to many of the interiors of the Shaker buildings in the village, like the way a boat was built; perfectly balanced. The overall Shaker village was impressive as it had been planned carefully and with great thought to its use and efficiency. Theirs was a tightly run ship indeed.

A Shaker workbench might be used for many years. Although worn with use, it was still of the same sturdy and useful character. With drawers and a cupboard with tools, it had its' own beauty and simple utility. Certainly so, for the Shaker cabinet maker.

In the Brethren's workshop building, there were rooms of useful space that accommodated various Shaker shops of industry. Yet, the types of industry had changed over the years. The Shaker brothers had ceased from making their own hats and shoes. The seed business had been discontinued and that shop was now used for the making rug whips. Some of the rooms were also used for storage. In one room were harvested potatoes and cabbages. During this time, an apple cellar had been built in the sub-basement of the building.

The windows of this workshop building brought in good and full sunlight during the day and yet, was altered in such ways as to create angular shadows that grew and faded with the position of the sun and the clouds. A rainstorm changed the light to something of a muted veil and on stormy days in any season, the stairways, halls and rooms could look gloomy and occupied by spirits. It held the past and hoped for the future. A fine structure that would accommodate both.

In the Mount Lebanon family dwelling kitchen were long useful surfaces for work. On the large stove were two hammered, shiny copper pots, circular and tall and with sturdy pointed lids with handles. Beneath the work surfaces were cabinets; doors concealing shelves for storage. On several of these shelves were a large set of new porcelain dishes with a design of a green border and small flowers. These with a superior quality of hardness and glaze surface and made by the American company of UPW (United Porcelain Works). The Church Family at Mount Lebanon was now nearly 70 in number and many dishes had been ordered to accommodate all Shakers. There were dinner plates, luncheon plates, bread plates, soup bowls, dessert bowls and cups and saucers. There were three sizes of oval serving bowls, large round serving bowls, syrup and water pitchers and relish plates.

On the wall of this kitchen was a rectangular Shaker clock and barometer and fixed to this same wall was an oil lamp. A gas light fixture hung from the ceiling and a Shaker ladder back chair rested up against a wall. The glass in the window's panes was mottled in clarity and gave a slightly distorted view. But it still gave accurate indication of the light in the sky and its' color on a particular day. In some ways, it was the best place in the house with its' cooking smells and plenty of heat from the stove. Even the fall or winter cold from an open door soon departed in this room with its' modern light and heat.

The Shaker sisters had brought in potatoes, onions and apples. These harvested from the gardens and placed on the work surface for trimming. In this season, it had become a daily task. Some of it would end up in one of the copper pots for soup.

There were rooms in the family dwelling houses for sleeping. It was simply furnished like all Shaker rooms. On a bedside table was a book of an unknown title and a pair of spectacles. On the walls were candle holders. A single rocker of a Shaker design rested on a hooked rug that covered the wood-plank floor. Once the sun set, the candles would be lit. A short reading and then rest from a long day's work.

A needle and thread were the tools made useful by Shaker sister hands in a room where fancy goods were made. In this room was a Shaker cabinet with several drawers. Most useful for storing buttons and threads and other sewing accessories. There were ladder-back chairs, a foot stool and a sewing machine. The window had no covering. The afternoon sunlight streamed through a window in that room, shifting subtly in intensity and indication. An edging shadow appearing where bright sunlight had been due to a cloud in the sky or the passing of the daylight hours. The work was slow and tedious. Sometimes accompanied by the singing of a Shaker song. Other times there was only silence in the room or the voices of the sisters in useful conversation. Heavenly angels kept watch over the Shaker sister's efforts, even though it was tied to earthly effects and needs. The Shaker sisters always mindful that all of it was for the demonstration and prosperity of the Mount Lebanon Shaker Community and its' mission of goodness over evil.

In the post American Civil War economy, the Shakers knew the value of their hand-made goods. In the new America, more and more machines of industry were used to manufacture and weave, to loom and to fabricate material goods. The Shaker-made product was synonymous with quality and fine craftsmanship. No one could duplicate their good work.

In the upstairs rooms of the family dwelling house were pleasant window views of valley land and the surrounding mountains. These mountains appearing as shades of different hues in the months of each season. Even black if a rain-storm or cloud-cover darkened the day enough. You could look out upon this land and witness the shifting rain clouds, listen to the thunder and witness the terrible flashes of lightening that appeared to strike the mountains. It always looked like a place of customs and legend. Of American mythology handed down as a tradition. Some of it lost, but much of it saved and adapted over generations. The Shakers recognized the spiritual connections here to the past. They felt it necessary to do so. Spirit séances were held to communicate with spirit friends. Written records were kept of such messages.

They greatly enjoyed nature. Shaker illustrations might be included with written words of spiritual encouragement. Such depictions within a letter, record book or a diary or represented in a hand-made item. A tree a symbol of life. A single leaf from that tree a thing of wonderment.

The Shakers had identified the different trees in the woods. As noted, in spring and summer, red oak tree leaves were a matte green with a blue-green underside. The leaves large and oval shaped with distinct sections ending in a point. Hickory tree bark was a silver-gray and with orange fissures. Its' leaves a dark-green with a paler underside. Its' wood strong and good for tool handles. There was the Eastern hemlock tree. Its' branching often near the ground on this tree. It had a brown-gray bark that also fissured with age. The pine-needle leaves a lighter green when young, then turning a dark green with maturity. Many tree species detailed in this way. Each tree had its' own unique beauty and stature.

Drawn against the sky by the setting sun or a morning sunrise in this hilly, Upstate New York State land.

The area of Mount Lebanon, New York was a useful place for farming. There was the natural spring water that flowed down from the distant mountains and surrounding hills. There was the sun, the wind and good, rich soil of the earth. It was a place for growing crops and for the grazing of animals. It was scenic but not in a dramatic way.

A great gold light appeared over the Appalachian hills that morning. It shined down on the land and made the trunks of trees seem like vertical shadows. Birds flew from their bare branches calling out to the sky. As the sun rose it improved all things and brought a bright sunlit day.

Here the earth told its' age. It could be wet and muddy in places. In other areas of land, it was dry and hard.

In their height, the surrounding hills seemed to hold a story. One waiting to be told. What remained here was tenuous and lively. Of Indian folklore and American founding.

All that day, a brilliant sunlight shone down onto the land. It seemed to diminish all shadows except at the narrowest corner and edge, both horizontal and vertical. It held everything in its place and reminded you of the usefulness of things and the value of a day's work. What was before you were the results of it, the daily upkeep and care of this prosperous and spiritual utopia. Grass was green and the wood houses painted white. There was stone and leaf, the rough bark of trees and the unfinished wood plank ready for sawing and staining. There was plowed soil, dust in the roads, mixed with a view of white clouds in the blue sky. There were the sounds of animals and industry, of well-water being pumped and the metal clang of a milk pail handle coming to rest for a moment. Voices might call out or there might be a conversation not quite overheard. It was a day at the Shaker village unexpected and not forecast in the Farmer's Almanac.

Cyryl Megalos was adjusting to his new environment. In his thoughts, he compared the land to the sea. He remembered that the sea made a soundless noise above the hastening of waves. Its' origin was youth but it was also old and wrinkled, dry and wet and briny. There was a different timbre on land; more of an echo and modified by the shifting

52

sun and the gathering moisture of rain. All of this he could not have verbally explained but he knew it, as he knew his own soul.

The Shaker brothers and Shaker sisters seemed equal here, at least in opinion and decision. Yet, like the weather or seasons, they seemed to know their time and place. There was an equality in communal living, property ownership, daily labor and the intellectual aspects of planning, decision making and the detailed expression of personal freedom. This idea of equality included race and gender. The Shakers valued people of color as no different in the eyes of God. They valued women as much as men, as God must, for were not they partnered as such in the Book of Genesis; in the Garden of Eden? Man and woman taking equal responsibility in the act of living here on earth.

There was a spiritual essence in striving for perfection in all that one accomplished. Cyryl thought this to be a result of old-fashioned ideas. The Shakers seemed obsessive in these matters of tasks and roles. They were strict but kind and patient. Time was not to be wasted. Theirs was a stern joyfulness in living. They were not at all Greek and Cyryl was sure of this. A Greek worked hard but also took joy in wine, song and the lustful expression of love. The history of the Greek was filled with folklore and mythology. The Greek was a poet, artist, a philosopher, a lover and appreciated all things of culture. The Greek was like no other human being on earth. The proof of this was in their fine statues and the artwork on the pottery they had made and in their classical literature that other nations had learned from and had copied; most obvious being the Romans. There had been the salvation of the Greek upon hearing the Christ story. Cyryl knew about all of this because he had been told this as a child. Not directly so much in an academic setting but through stories of Greece and Greek relatives. He had also learned a lot about Greek history and art from his visit to the Boston museum. These Shaker people were not Greek but originated from Northern Europe and now America. He still was not sure what to think of them and their communal way of life. They seemed kind and yet sparingly so.

"A day is a gift from God," said Shaker Brother Matthew. "We take that day and we make something of it. We don't think of the weather; cloudy or a day of sunshine. The value of it we create by our actions and conduct." He was speaking to the workmen. It was a chance meeting and

Shaker Brother Matthew took the opportunity to comment on the value of a day's work. Above all things the Mount Lebanon Shaker Village was a place of hard work and reverence to God. Prayer meetings were held at the Shaker Meeting House. The human soul was often a topic of discussion amongst the Shaker Society members. The separation of good and evil had commenced.

Cyryl and Stephen had not been around such religious people before and so they usually kept a polite distance from them. Sometimes the Shaker brothers or sisters seemed too stern and rigorous in their manner or self-expression. Stephen thought they lacked a sense of humor. But they were learned in the ways of farming and the making of tools and useful objects such as furniture, cabinetry and textiles. They were simple, plain, hard-working people and relentless in their pursuit of perfection. Cyryl wanted to learn all he could from them. He wanted a farm and he wanted it to be prosperous enough to support himself and a family. He listened to their instruction. He kept quiet unless he was spoken to. Idle talk seemed to bother the Shakers. Most conversation involved a task or reference to God and the lord savior, Christ Jesus. But they were all different as people are. They had their own personalities that shown through in the way they greeted you or related a story or instruction. He would learn that they were not above humor and they took joy in the act of daily living.

The early morning sky above was gray and the daylight dim. The trees had lost their leaves. A stronger wind shook their bare branches.

Another day announced itself. A bright sunlight lit the roof of the North Family house. Smoke from its' chimney mixed with the frigid air rising to a pale blue sky. Only two billowy white clouds equally spaced were seen in the sky. Breakfast was being prepared in the kitchen. If you were to look inside, the contents of the Shaker family house cupboard included many ceramic dishes, a soup tureen with ladle, and Pennsylvania made glassware. There was a cut-glass bowl and matching water pitcher given as a gift to the Shakers that was only used for special dinners.

A breakfast of oatmeal and bread with jam was eaten. The morning work was commenced and completed. An afternoon overcast sky seemed closer to the earth that day; the Appalachian land still green in places.

Despite the colder weather, the important water irrigation project for the workmen continued at the Shaker community. Shaker Brother Matthew now examined the aerial plans of the Shaker village and the irrigation system. The recent changes made in pencil to this vast system documented on drafting paper had been placed over the original plans. New buildings and revised area of land usage had been added or noted. No one had taught Shaker Brother Matthew how to adapt these drawings. He had done this himself. The Shaker brothers had learned the art of hand drafting and the meticulous work of accurate planning and revising of plans had been self-taught. It was the same with the great architecture of the village, merely conceived as to its' symmetry and remarkable design. Past architectural styles were referenced and modified.

The Shakers had emerged as true innovators in all the industries they took upon themselves as a means of profit. They were remarkably creative people. But it was their spiritual fervor that really was the origin of their perfection of all things and their utopian village and material goods only a reflection of their faith in their savior, Christ the Lord. They would readily remind you of it as you admired something they had to sell. They were not the goods they sold, only the hands that represented the work of God.

As for the Shakers, what was within their rooms, in the buildings they constructed, were a means to a utopian place on earth. With objects of function and utility; chairs that when not in use were hung upside down from pegs on the walls. They floated in the shadows and light of early morning day and late evening. There was a simplicity and mirror-like symmetry in the architectural design of Shaker interiors that lifted the ordinary to something spiritual, and seen in their unique and reasoned approach to the materials from which to build; given to them by God. Through their application of the spiritual in the physical manifestation of a building, they had somehow created heaven; ethereal interior space in shape, appearance and plan.

At this hour, the Shaker sisters in the North Family house were in a room sewing and reading before going to their beds to sleep. An oil lamp on a table illuminated the pages of the bible and gave enough light to keep the knitting needles in one sister's hands moving in their repeated motions. The rows of color of a Shaker braided rug on the floor, green, blue, gold and orange glowed in the light of the oil lamp. Its' flame made the shadow of the table jump and pull at an angle. The oil lamp itself was a magnified reflection on the wall. The strong wind outside could be heard whistling. There was a window view of branches and their leaves being tossed in the night wind.

"I think we ought to go to bed sisters," said a Shaker sister.

And with that they took the burning oil lamp and left the room in darkness. The day had ended.

There was something singular and peaceful in the following day. It was as short as the life of a butterfly and long as a lifetime. It was an ordinary day filled with the wonder of God and all he had created; men and women, the animals that helped sustain us, the good and fertile fields and wooded land. If one could look down at this place from the sky it would look calm and orderly. The fields and sensibly planned buildings on measured plots of land. It had grown from the very land, the spirit of the land and even the sky that sometimes resembled the land in its' cloud formations and color. Shades marked it as well; bright white or gray or a luminous sky-blue reflection in land water.

It was at present a Wednesday night. The singing of a song by Shaker voices could be heard coming from the Shaker Meeting House. The faint movement of dancing feet on the hard-plank wood floor above echoed from inside the building along with their voices. Like all spiritual music heard from inside a place of worship, it sounded ethereal and yet, it was the most human of sounds possible. It was joyful in a muted way, in a way that reflected steadiness and personal satisfaction. Within the meeting room itself, the sounds of Shaker voices and dancing feet would be much louder, at times almost thunderous. The Shakers were in a certain kind of ecstasy during this time of worship; their spiritual energy building to a physical force of power.

Cyryl and Stephen now spoke with a Shaker brother. It was this brother that, in manner, gave the final approval of the hiring of a new employee.

"What is your name?" he asked Cyryl.

"It is Cyryl Megalos."

"That's a noble sounding name. Are you of Greek descent?" asked the Shaker brother.

"My parents were Greek," said Cyryl.

"And you want to stay and work here with us for a time? Why is that, young man? Are you unhappy in the life you have made?" asked the Shaker brother.

"I have made my living from the sea. I have been a fisherman like my father. But now I wish to become a farmer. I want to work on land," said Cyryl.

"Are you honest and a hard worker? Do you love Christ?" asked the Shaker brother.

"I am honest and hard working. I have never taken to drink. I have only thought of Christ when I was in peril of losing my life," said Cyryl.

"Well, that's a narrow view of the Lord. But we don't require you to have faith as us. You seem mindful of the lord, in your own way," said the Shaker brother.

"Yes, sir." said Cyryl, wanting to show respect.

"And you sir, I have heard you seem to be honest and a good worker." He was speaking to Stephen, who had remained still and polite in his manner.

"Was your father a farmer son?" asked the Shaker brother.

"No, he was a laborer at a local mill, sir in the city of Boston. I worked on farms during my summers growing up in Massachusetts," said Stephen.

"Well then, the fall season work is over and the harvest is finished, but not completely. You will have to help us with the rest of it. And we have many things to keep you busy. You will earn your keep. And perhaps you will learn enough of farming to give you a better start of it. This is good land here but it is varied. Some fields fertile for crops and others not so very much. It can be stony and full of clay. There is often stones in these fields," said the Shaker brother.

Cyryl and Stephen listened to the Shaker brother as he went on about the geographical aspects of the Mount Lebanon land. They felt great relief knowing they would have shelter for the winter months.

Cyryl's idea of farming seemed a real possibility. He had not led his friend Stephen Blome astray. He would find a piece of land of his own. It would have fertile soil, free of clay and stone. And it would have trees, trees that would bear fruit, just like in the Garden of Eden. It was a story his mother had told him as a young boy, a green, jungle-forest of a place with flowers and fruit trees.

"You have not asked me where I am from; what town or place," said Cyryl.

"God has brought you to us. In what town have you lived?" asked the Shaker brother.

"I have lived in city of Boston, Massachusetts, most recently, although my parents first arrived in New York City and we lived on the Lower East Side with many other immigrant families," said Cyryl.

The Shaker brother seemed impressed with Cyryl and Stephen. They seemed bright and intelligent. Superior fishermen they seemed. The biggest problem with the hired workers were those men that had quick tempers or concealed a bad character or a drinking habit. Cyryl and Stephen seemed to be above all this.

The brother interviewed Stephen Blome more purposely. He found him sincere and he looked strong and healthy. He fidgeted in front of the Shaker brother though, and so he did not seem as comfortable in his surroundings as Cyryl, the Greek American. Stephen had stated that he had been raised in a Christian home. At least this was what he told the Shaker brother. The details he gave of this Christian faith were somewhat vague, but the brother did not press too strongly on this point of personal history. The Shaker brother had told both men that they must be sober and reliable, good hard workers and always honest in their communication with others. The two men had work for the winter months and possibly longer.

That following day all Shakers were busy with a task. Even as late as the season was, the Shaker sisters tended to the garden picking beans and squash, while Shaker brothers nearby brought in beets from a field. Hired workmen repaired a wagon or saddled horses for a journey into town. Indoors the industry of busy hands carved and mended or measured a piece of wood for precise cutting. And yet, there were times during the day when all Shakers were unseen or indoors. They had disappeared indoors for prayer or a meal, or the time and circumstance of the day had made them simply unseen. Some people thought the Shaker to be an odd sort of individual. A Shaker brother or sister had been known to writhe and shake and fall to the ground while being possessed by the holy spirit. They had been known to speak in tongues at any hour of the day. They were known for their dancing and clapping during their meetings of worship. These could be uniform rows of Shaker dancers or Shakers forming a great circle or circles. These circles were often homogeneous in gender. Some of the Shaker men were old and had the face of a Moses or a hollowed eyed preacher. Other men were stunningly handsome and youthful, yet almost melancholy in their seated position while in worship. The women too, could be handsome or as plain as could be, but a love of God seemed to radiate in their hearts, whether seen in the expression of their face or in the tone of their singing voices. They were as human as could be, yet they strived to be more like Christ in their utopian place where the separation of good and evil had begun for the preparation of the lord's final return.

And too, the thriving Shaker community was a peaceful place and the Shakers were not confrontational people in the least. On the contrary, they greatly valued the ideals of freedom and peace. Their early history in America was quite different. They had been looked upon as eccentric and even a threat to traditional Christian faith, in that their way of life was anything but based on the idea of a traditional family unit. Seen as a communistic religious cult, the Shakers had been met with much violence; mobs of angry citizens had attacked many a Shaker prior to the protection of their communities. There was safety in numbers and their membership had grown considerably since founder Mother Ann Lee had first began her mission to gather believers. They had not only survived but they had thrived on, to become respected American citizens, inventors and prosperous entrepreneurs.

The Shakers could now see what they had accomplished but there was always the challenge to stay a thriving community of believers. They were an American singularity born from their unique interpretation of the

Christian faith. Like something organic in its' manifestation, their communities had grown larger and prosperous. Yet, how non-traditional their ways were; shunning the family unit for a spiritual community place of celibate and separated gender members. Utopian in its' character; making it odd in its' American reputation and endeavor. The produced results of their work from fine architecture to simple garden seeds were notable. And their neighboring citizens recognized in these people a superior accomplishment unattained within the usual social and spiritual setting.

That evening Shaker Brother Matthew's walking shadow blew out the candle in his room. Once in bed, he prayed for his soul in case death should take him during the night hours. He arose the next morning and it was the sunlight that created a different sort of shadow in his room. He thanked his lord for another day of life.

That following afternoon Stephen heard something he had not heard before during a daytime. Stephen could hear singing from the Shaker Meeting House. He didn't think himself very religious. He wasn't a Shaker and he felt oddly isolated from them at that moment. His childhood memories of religious faith, were very different from this Shaker place. But he felt lucky because he was in a good place, safe and clean and separate from the often unfair and counterfeit dealings of the world. It was an eccentric place, though.

Cyryl believed in destiny. He was destined to be there at the Shaker village. Where he would have ended up that winter he couldn't imagine; out of work possibly and out of money. Christ must have brought him to this place for a reason, and he believed that Christ must have seen him traveling away from the sea and had guided his way. He remembered his work as a fisherman as being exhausting. There were tiring days when he didn't notice the weather or the time. Only a vague conception of morning or afternoon as a rain fell or the sun shone relentlessly. It was a poor trade, one of the poorest and he wondered why his father had taken it up like his father before. There was something in his Greek soul that had told him it was tradition and honorable. It was his place in a world, where a man's place meant something. Often it was tied to the past and to a heritage of a family. To do better was something good, but usually a large increase in wealth or good luck was a gift from God for good actions and the result of prayer. Luck was something you could pray for but a small blessing was more likely. The fact that he had found the courage to move on to something else, was a miracle unto itself. It meant that he had found it in his own soul to search for something better. Part of the reason was this country America, that offered new frontiers and opportunity for all.

That night Cyryl could not sleep and so he put on his trousers and shirt and went outside of the workman's building. It was cold and the quietest night Cyryl had ever listened to with such keen ears. There was no sound to be heard at all, but Cyryl thought he heard music; a music from the past. Perhaps the origin of it was a time when he was a child. This place America was his home now, but a part of it would always be foreign. This was because of the stories his parents had told him of Greece and his relatives there.

He had a memory of his mother. The two of them, Cyryl and his mamma, were together and shopping for food. Black olives, bread, Feta cheese, sausages and a bottle of wine for papa. There were good smells and bad smells in New York City. Bread smelled good and the roses they sold in a bunch alongside the vegetables and fruits. The narrow, crowded streets smelled bad and the garbage that was left to rot in the sun. On one occasion, he had seen another part of New York; nicer streets that did not smell, with trees and horse and carriages that carried well-to-do ladies and gentlemen to their important destinations or for a stroll in the park. That was his memory of the past. Such a dark place it seemed that night, this American Shaker dwelling. Something had brought him here and he thought it a curious destiny. But there he was and he would live it day to day until that same motivation in his heart would lead him to another place.

Shaker Sister Rebecca has been adopted by the Shakers at an early age. Shaker Sister Rebecca's mother had died. Her father, a Methodist minister, had become a Shaker himself and then he had left her in the care of the Shakers upon his own death. There had been no close relatives except an aunt who did not seem confident enough to care for the young girl. She had many memories of her father. She remembered his lessons and books. He was a philosopher and spoke well when called upon. He had a talent for preaching and expressing intelligent thoughts. She was only nine when her father passed away. It was a difficult time for her and she escaped to the world of books and learning. This is how she came to be a teacher at the Shaker village school of Mount Lebanon. She was a very pretty girl, with light blonde hair and blue eyes, so pretty that the Shaker men and women warned her of the dangers of vanity. A pure and loving soul outshined any pretty face. But often she was told what a blessing she was to the Shaker village. God had brought Rebecca to them for a reason.

Shaker Sister Rebecca took off her cap that evening and looked in the mirror above the wash basin. She was a pretty, young girl. She knew she wasn't vain about it, but only aware of her own physical prettiness. The Shaker sisters had told her so as well, and laughingly told her not to let it give her pretenses about herself. Beauty was found in all things that God had made. She was to make herself modest in appearance and reflect an obedience to the lord. In the eyes of our creator God, men and women were equal. It was something that the outside civilized world seemed to have forgotten in some ways. Women were mistrusted in matters of finance and labor. The Shakers knew better. All men and women had an equal hand in God's work.

She remembered when she was a young child and getting angry at her parents for leaving her all alone. She knew they were dead but still, she insisted that they return to ask for her forgiveness. She would wait for the rest of an hour. And yet, no one entered the room and she brushed a tear aside. This was life was to be like she had told herself, large and small disappointments and with only Jesus Christ and his salvation as a comfort.

III

Winter Approaches

Autumn had brought its' colors. Yet, some trees had remained green like the pine trees in the hills. Along the Shaker fields, there were bare oak trees. On the ground below were acorns and dry leaves still vibrant in their altered hue.

If you were to walk in the wooded areas in autumn as a Shaker brother might, upon inspection, there would be tree leaves mottled or spotted in color; blotchy yellow, blue-green and even black. The fall wind would lift the fallen foliage up and show their colors in the sunlight or on a cloudy day. Their wind-swept sound a crisp echo; as if a recollection of seasons past. Approaching nightfall reduced them to a noise beneath your walking feet. A reminder of impending winter.

At the Shaker village, the work of the harvest was complete and the ground was often covered by a frost on any given morning. There were still days when the sun would warm the earth as if striving for a different season. The dry, brittle leaves that covered the ground announced a sleeping of the land that would soon take place. A few great maple and oak leaves still hung from branches waiting to fall. But most of the magnificent color of fall had turned to browns; crisp and curling leaves mixed with broken twigs from branches and the dust from the earth.

A Shaker brother had died that early morning; Shaker Brother Malias. It was before he had risen for daily labor. It cast a shadow over the community that day and into the evening. He had been beloved by all. He had been elderly but in fair health. Natural causes were the decided reason. He had said the closing prayer the night before at the prayer meeting. His voice had trembled as it always had as he thanked Jesus Christ for his always present love and forgiveness. He had studied botany as a hobby and he knew much about the growing of herbs and trees, their leaf shapes and the way useful plants should be tended all year-round. He had kept a record of all he had learned on bound pages of paper with his own meticulous drawings. How beautifully the leaves and stems and blooms had been rendered in ink with rarely a blotch or noticeable error in their estimated dimension. He had been particularly dear to the Shaker sisters for his help with the garden and with his special kind ways.

"A fine man and an agreeable man is Shaker Brother Malias," they had often said. The opposite of the stern and irritable Shaker Brother Podd.

Shaker Brother Podd was a different kind of character. If one were to be honest in their account, Shaker Brother Podd seemed as dry as dead weed in late fall. His disposition was humorless and his thoughts always on some dilemma or unseen obstacle. He often spoke of the unfailing love of Christ and his power of salvation. Yet, he lacked any sustained spiritual joy and you wondered what life event had brought him to such a vinegary attitude. This man as a young boy seemed a remote possibility and what had overtaken his spirit to place him in such a stern and tasteless appearance seemed outside of any spiritual cause. He was unpleasant to be tact and the other Shaker members treated him with respect, but often grew more careful in their conversation when in his presence. To Shaker Brother Podd, idle talk was of the devil. A godly attitude allowed for very little discussion of obvious labor and daily acts of devotion. There were many Shaker brothers and sisters close in manner to Shaker Brother Podd; overall, stern and one might say, humorless in their attitude and appearance. It was Shaker Brother Podd, though, that had cultivated a nature of almost sour reprehension. Even a Shaker could only take him in small doses like castor oil or a homemade remedy for something that ailed, made of dandelion stems and the bitterest of roots and herbs.

It was another workday. Inside the Great Stone Barn, sunlight streamed in from the rows of windows. The movement of the clouds affecting the measure of this sunlight. Several of the workmen including Cyrl did their assigned work there that day. It was day and yet, inside this large stone structure it was night striving to be day. It represented something like faith; the idea of it as a choice and something to strive for.

64

On another day in this early winter season, Cyryl and the other workmen entered the edge of the woods from the road. Frost was still on the ground from the early morning. The day had not warmed and winter was announcing its' arrival with this day of a much colder temperature and a gray sky. The underbrush and land was a dark blue under these trees, a shadow melded into one shade, dark and even. A distance from where they had entered the woods, they came to small land opening and a group of trees, separate and near the road. The men stopped for a moment to look at them. The trees seemed different from any other in the wooded area. Perhaps it was because they were physically separate. The land they grew on was a slight hill. Their trunks and brown branches seem to hold the season within their leafless reach like no other trees. Bits of green moss could be seen on their rough, bark trunks. They were old trees but not more than a century, for their age could be told in their slenderness and color. Very old trees took on a more majestic look that was almost furrowed or gnarled in a way only very old trees could appear in their physical result. The men headed down the road and back to the workmen's dwelling house. A few leaves from trees fell to the ground and the wind lifted them as they rose from the ground in light swirls.

That late November day turned from blue sky to gray with snow falling by late afternoon. It was a light snowfall that seemed to come from heaven as if to transform all things on earth into a white, clean place. The absence of wind made the snow fall as if feathering to the land below; dusting the bare branches of trees now half white with it. The absence of daylight, dimming to early evening left the fallen snow another color, a sort of shadowed white, silent in its' accomplishment.

The following day the dried weeds in nearby fields were now covered in frost and snow. The birds looked for seed on the snow-covered ground. Seed that had blown from the dried stalks of plants that would scatter such pips on a winter afternoon. Their small descending shapes landing where they might find this scarce fare near the withered underbrush and trees or in a harvested field.

Snow now filled the air. Cyryl had to walk across one of these fields to a Shaker building. He looked about him as the falling snowflakes quickly accumulated onto the land and was caught in the brown leaves

65

and divided stems of the weeds. The white of snow left the underbrush stranded in this cover. He wondered what the outdoor mercury thermometer read at that moment. It had grown much colder from the day before and the sky above was now a darker shade of gray. It was one of those winter days when day would never fully come; as if the overcast sky would not allow it, hiding the sun and holding a part of day as night.

It was on this day that Cyryl saw the ill-humored Shaker Brother Podd for the first time. He stood alone near a frozen field looking out at it and when he saw Cyryl in his stride, he gazed at him directly with the coldest look a man had ever directed towards young Cyryl. Cyryl stopped for a moment and returned the man's inquiring look. He thought himself in a trouble of some sort but then the old Shaker man looked away from him, then out at the field, and then began a walk towards one of the family houses without speaking. He had seemed a part of the cold landscape, an apparition of it or an attachment to it, somehow crafted from the ice and snow and the dead wood of winter.

That evening good food and the light of an oil lamp was shared by the workmen. The men were more conscious of the warmth of indoors as the season had grown colder. Stories were told and music sung or played on musical instruments. The hired workers were treated well here at Mount Lebanon. Whether they really liked the place or not was another matter.

Workmen Cyryl, Stephen, Bill and Ned sat eating their meal. Outdoors and visible through a window, the sun was setting a rose pink. At first, they were all silent being hungry and tired, but soon a conversation commenced.

"I think of when I was a fisherman, said Cyryl. "My hands are still rough from handling the rope nets".

"And the cuts on your hands would sting when you had them in salty sea water. I started wearing gloves but it still didn't take away the stinging from the tiny cuts on my hands," said Stephen.

"I would get tired of the hot sun but then on a cloudy day, I sometimes wished for it. When it rained, it brought changes to the sea. The fish seemed to grow scarce as if no longer drawn to the sun reflecting on the surface of the water. The fishing was best on days when the wind was low and there was sunshine. I listened to the sea," said Cyryl.

"I think the sea was driving you mad, Cyryl", said Stephen,

"Perhaps it was. I am glad to be away from it," said Cyryl.

Next, Bill spoke.

"This is a pretty place but not as pretty as where I grew up in Pennsylvania," said Bill. He sounded homesick.

"This is more valley land though and better for crops. Where I grew up in Pennsylvania, the land is half covered with trees; a whole lot of pine trees and lakes. "Where is it you said you grew up?" asked Ned. He rose and stretched his body.

"I am from Northern Pennsylvania, the Scranton area," said Bill.

Bill continued his talk about Pennsylvania. Ned walked away from the table. Often, he separated himself like this from the other men. After eating a bowl of oat porridge, he leaned against the stairwell wall and rested his head. He held the empty bowl and spoon in his hands. The look on his face was one of quiet acceptance.

Cyryl found him sitting there alone on the steps.

"Ned, are you ok?" said Cyryl.

"I am ok," said Ned. He had come to life again and was on his feet after a struggle to bring himself upright while balancing the bowl and spoon.

"What were you thinking about?" asked Cyryl.

"Children, said Ned. I miss being around children. I don't have any of my own. I love children," said Ned.

"Well, there is always the possibility for those," said Cyryl. "Just find a pretty lady and marry her."

"Yes, but which pretty lady?" asked Ned.

"I am sure you will meet her one day. We had better head upstairs and get some sleep," said Cyryl.

"Cyryl, you are the most confident man I have ever met," said Ned.

"There is no reason for you to think poorly of yourself, Ned," said Cyryl.

That night in Appalachia came the first real snowfall. By the light of morning, the fields had been transformed to white. The sky had changed as well. It was a winter sky of orange and gray. The Appalachian hills that morning a darker shade.

Two months prior the leaves from the trees had shook in the breeze. Chestnuts and green walnuts found among fallen leaves and branches on the ground. Now all was hidden except for the brown remnants of fall and that previous summer.

That day, as usual, the small movements of labor by hand accomplished tasks that reflected the value of patience and perfection in the production of a chair, a box or the section of a Shaker quilt. It was a quiet employment that contributed to the overall profit of a community that had thrived and become rich in its reputation of producing fine goods and usable items of human consumption and use.

Another day had ended. The sun was setting outside and the Shaker sisters were in their kitchen preparing a dinner of cooked chicken, potatoes and green beans. There would be apple pie with cream for dessert. In this family house kitchen, it was better to prepare what they could before nightfall; which required the use of candles or kerosene lamps. They knew the seasons and when the approximate time that daylight would fade in the sky and dusk would replace it. Shadows would appear and leave a visual stillness in all things that was expressed in blank, shadowy surface. There were days when they found themselves ahead or behind this useful light of day. Ordinary things like apples or the print of a tablecloth would suddenly fade to a colorless hue and unseen texture. The candle or clean-burning kerosene lamp would re-light the darkness and make these things seem fuller in depth as if in a still-life painting. The background of a room darker and the candle or lamp light limited to the area in which it illuminated. The light from several candles had its own symbolism here; the collective light creating a brighter illumination and showing that there is a power in unity and goodness. God had given them night and day as symbols of good and evil. To the Shakers, Christ the lord illuminated the entire world with his light and promise of eternal life.

IV

The Winter Shaker

The sunrise was gold and orange in the trees. The sky above dispelling night. Snow still seen in patches on the land now exposed. The dried leaves there from the previous fall.

It seemed strange to Cyryl that he was in this Mount Lebanon, New York valley. He put on his fisherman's cap and a long wool scarf and headed outdoors to his work. He looked out at the surrounding mountains. His feet stood on solid ground. He felt close to the land as his work often involved the land. As the son of Greek immigrants, he had never felt more at home in America. It was the learning that was important to Cyryl. Everyday brought the opportunity for it. He felt as if he could now farm and even make things like the Shakers. It was all in your attitude and consistent hard work. And not so different from fishing or any other field of work.

His friend Stephen seemed to like this new life as well. He had expressed contentment with the consistency of his circumstances. It was hard work but your pay was guaranteed. There were no unprofitable days, due to overfishing or bad weather. He felt a conventional fellow at last and it showed in his clothes; a new canvas coat, new Levi overalls and lighter weight cotton shirts that kept him cooler out-of-doors. He rarely wore the navy-blue wool coat he had brought with him that identified him as a fisherman and a sailor. He smiled more and he told jokes and he commented on the good meals provided. It was a relief for Cyryl who felt responsible for the success of their inland journey to find work. His intuition had proved him correct. Neither of them seemed to miss the sea.

In definition, at least according to the Shakers, Cyryl was not a "Winter Shaker," but simply a hired workman. A "Winter Shaker" was someone who came for a season to work with the Shakers and to also

69

live closely with them. There was the possible intention of becoming a Shaker; a spiritual consideration. This was not Cyryl's (or Stephen's) intention. But Cyryl who had always had a strong sense of his own spiritual being and destiny, was in all respects the same, as he felt something had brought him to this place to learn and to grow as he should. In this regard, he too was a "Winter Shaker," in following his heart to this place of great spiritual purpose and destiny.

It was snowing flurries that day. The boughs of green and blue evergreen were now heavy with it. It clung to the bark and branches of the trees. A horse and carriage brought cans of milk and cream to one of the family houses. It would stop at every house and then return to the dairy barn. The sky was a hazy gray above and the snow seemed to fall from nowhere but appear as if by magic once it was close to the land. It was now December and the ground a frozen landscape of white and brown. As far as one could see the light snow floated to the ground; shapes of white on the ground rising higher. Later that morning Cyryl shook a branch of a spruce pine tree. The snow on its' laden branch flew in the wind and wet his face. Snow looked different in the city; a white edging of things or a clean cover on the ground, that quickly changed to a muddy-brown slush. This country snow remained white and was only interrupted on the ground by underbrush left exposed above its drifts. It was a clean snow and if you looked closely you would see its flakes sparkling with the colors of the spectrum. In the fields, taller brown stalks of dried weeds obtruded above the snow drifts curved and lopsided. The barks of the trees along the fields were crusted white in places. The branches of the trees a tangle of white web. The sounds of bird calls filled the air. A flash of red meant a Cardinal. Black was a crow. Sparrows and other birds flew from branch to branch tossing off the caught snow. At midday, the sunlight cast a thin, yellow light onto the snow-covered field. Its' glare partially hid your view of the forest edge and it made the land shine in places.

The Shaker village slept that winter night. All was dark and barely seen in a moonlight that made light shadows on the snow-covered ground. The weather had turned much colder.

The Mount Lebanon Shaker Village in its' present state, was impressive to see and there were many visitors. For this very reason, the Shaker sisters had opened a Shaker store and gift shop where Shaker goods were sold. Within the valley, there were many buildings that supported the community's domestic, industrial and agricultural needs including the ministry house and the main dwelling both of which showed a Victorian style of architectural influence. There was a building where chairs were made, the North Family's Stone Barn, the older First Meeting House and the newer Second Meeting House with its arched roof and five entryways, with the left door for Shaker brothers, the middle for Shaker elders, the right for Shaker sisters. And two on the East side for non-Shakers. Seed production, patent medicines and chair manufacturing were among the many profitable commercial businesses that sustained the community. With the decline of male members, workers and craftsmen and women had been hired to keep these businesses profitable and viable.

Not all men laborers hired by the Shakers worked out as well as Cyryl and Stephen. Others were sent packing for drinking liquor or starting fights. There were accusations of stealing and foul language. But for the most part it was a harmonious group of men that needed work and were grateful for their place at the Shaker community.

The workmen that remained now headed outdoors for work. The partial sunlight on the snow made it look blue that day. The shadows of things longer. The bare tree branches that edged the snow-covered fields of crop stubble were a tangle of black, thin branches. Patches of ice covered the ground under the trees and reflected a white sunlight. It made the ice on the branches of the trees glisten in places. Otherwise, the wooded landscape was mostly bare trees and snow-covered weeds.

The day's work was ending and the workmen were walking back to their residence across a flat section of land that was covered with pine cones and clumps of green needles that had broken off from the tall pine trees. The day was growing dim and a sunset was now almost gone along the horizon. It showed the vertical shapes of tree trunks and their branches for a few minutes and then the trees became a gray shapeless cloud.

71

Here in New York State, in a farming–type community, Cyryl was living the life of a farmer. Well, a hired hand was what he was referred to as being, but it was as close as he had come to experiencing work on a farm in a country place. Stephen Blome seemed more familiar with the workings of a farm. Appalachia was a good place with rich valley soil and pretty mountain scenery all around. Green fields edged with white birch and elm Trees. Wildflowers grew in the fields and along the dirt roads.

The Shakers were a unique people and along with being hard-working they enjoyed themselves as well. There were dinners and Sunday lunches, birthdays and holidays were celebrated in their own way. They could be stern and then too, good-humored. They seemed to love their lives and their God more than anything else. This earthly place could be a heavenly one too, but a temporary one. Appalachia suited them well.

Ned was a hired workman like Cyryl and Stephen. He had been with the Shaker's for several seasons, arriving like Cyryl at the start of a Winter. He was a slight handsome fellow of medium height and color, and he had a limp and a slightly twisted torso. Even with his disability, he was a strong and consistent worker. He said his physical abnormality was from a childhood injury, but the other workmen thought he had been born with the disability. He hid his slight frame with a pair of baggy pants that was held up with suspenders. His baggy work shirt rolled up to his elbows, added a size to his strong but narrow biceps and shoulders. He had the heart of a child and all the workmen had taken a liking to him. He was a little brother; a true friend. His hard work was always undeniable and he always seemed grateful for his place at the Shaker village. You could imagine why he had ended up at a place like the Shaker village. He was too good for the world in an obvious way. A world that could take little pity on a person different in attitude or physicality. And had beat nearly to death many a Shaker believer for his or her unconventional religious belief and unshakable stance. Ned would stay at the Shaker Village and then go off for the summer months only to return in the early fall. Some said he rented a room in nearby New Lebanon and went fishing. Others thought he had family but he never wished to speak of them. Perhaps he feared that if he revealed too much of his circumstances, he might lose his seasonal position at the Shaker village. He liked ghost stories and he thought them to be lost souls in search of salvation or a way to heaven. And he liked tales of the Indians. Pioneer explorers also excited him and he retold many stories of these men and women after an evening meal. He read the New Testament Bible and he seemed to have a good knowledge of this holy book and the symbolism through its' lessons. He had been taught these stories at a country church where no music was ever played on instruments or on a piano. Only the voices of its' congregants were allowed. It was something he remembered because it spoke of the kind of spiritual reverence he had witnessed as a young boy. He remembered sitting on a wooden church bench looking out of a window that was not covered with stain glass but revealed the green leaves of a tree. Jesus the Lord was there with them and the tree leaves that moved in the wind or changed in color or in illuminated size comforted him somehow. He thought his work should be out-of-doors when possible and he had told this to the Shakers.

There was workman, Bill Patterson, the sturdy, tall young man from Pennsylvania. Bill looked like a man from Pennsylvania and that was the only way to describe him. He was strong looking with dark brown hair, bright blue eyes, large hands and broad shoulders. He was as strong and solid as a mature pine tree. He was Eastern American in his manner and style; this being a mixture of rural and urban sensibility that came from the reading of newspapers and visits as a child to relatives in Pittsburgh and Philadelphia. He was casual in his manner, manly and unaffected. He wore plaid shirts and Levi jeans and he folded his clothes and cared for his few belongings with the utmost of care. He seemed to have mixed feelings about the Shakers and he had an audacious sense of humor that sometimes targeted the actions of the Shaker brothers and sisters. But it was a respectful observance on his part. His humor always included good words as well, such as descriptions of "sweet" or "fussy" but never of the disrespectful sort. He was a protestant in faith but these Shakers were Christ followers of another kind; too extreme in their separate ways and peculiarities. Back home, Bill had started to drink and then quit. He was good at sports like football but was too restless and he admitted to being a "bad kid" when growing up." But he seemed to have found his way. He was saving his money. He would return home and take over his father's half-farm. Half-farm meaning it was on the edge of a small central Pennsylvania town. His dad also worked part of the time at a local steel mill. He had two brothers and a sister. They were all younger. They looked up to Bill. Bill knew he had to do his best.

John Michael was also a workman hired by the Shakers. He was an African-American who had been born to slaves in Georgia. He did not know if his brother was still alive but he knew that his mother and father and an older sister still resided and worked on a Georgia farm. It was in Eastern Georgia, a scenic place near the ocean where he had been raised as a child. His mother and father, he thought, although free, still had the mindset of slaves and thinking of it angered him at times. He of course loved them and he wished for them something better. His older sister had married and she too, had remained on a farm in this area of Georgia. John Michael loved learning and books, but his favorite was, as he thought it should be, the Holy Bible. John Michael now approached the age of forty. He had piercing black eyes. His hair had grown gray at the temples. His face had a noble, oval shape not unlike the wood boxes the Shakers assembled from thin bent wood pieces latched together with lids in descending sizes. He was still unmarried, but he had courted for a good while now an African-American woman in the town of New Lebanon. His lady friend worked as a housekeeper and nanny to a white family. Why John Michael had not asked her to marry was not discussed. It was a source of a joke among the workmen; when John was heading out to meet up with her for another evening of courting.

"When are you going to marry that woman, John?" asked a workman.

"She'll know soon enough," said John Michael. "No use in rushing things as I see it. I am not sure she and I like each other that good. She is disagreeable and I can be as stubborn as a mule."

John Michael had laughed at his own remark. He nodded his head in agreement to his talk. He was a man of little learning but what he had learned he had put to heart. He thought the Shakers to be very good people and prophets. His brother had disappeared during the American Civil War and it was believed he had either escaped to the North successfully or he had met his death in doing so. John Michael thought him most likely dead but he had not given up hope in seeing him alive someday. He often prayed to God for this miracle but it had never come. He would look up from his work in the field and look for his brother Josiah, but he had never appeared. He would see him in heaven, a Shaker brother had predicted, yes, in heaven.

The Shakers made and used candles and kerosene lamps for their interior rooms. Outside of that glow of the lamp or candle the darkness was pitch black; a darkness out-of-doors that brought the star-filled night sky close to the earth. A candle seemed a spiritual light cast against the walls of the Shaker houses. It drew out shadows of ladder-back chairs or the exaggerated form of a hanging apron of a Shaker sister floating and trembling.

The words of holy scripture heard in the candlelight and against the dark of evening, seemed a spiritual beacon against all evil and uncertainty. For iniquity was there lurching, to oppose goodness and well-being. Waiting in the shadows of things to overtake the hearts and minds of Christ's devoted followers.

If ghosts were about they might be colonial New Englanders, mountain dwellers, travelers; of Indian tribes. Their spiritual presence a part of the land shadows reaching from the mountain forests; the timber and force of the wind during any season; seen as the quick glimpse of a visage wearing a coat and hat, or in a dress with a flowing skirt. But this community of Christian faith and spiritual power was one of peace and reconciliation with God. Any ghostly spirit of a restless entity would most certainly recede back to the origin of which it came.

The next morning would bring the daylight gray and dim or streaming white and bright through the windows of the houses. To the Shakers, it was God's salvation coming forth to redeem the sinner from his lonely journey outside of the light of God and his son, Jesus Christ.

There were children at the Shaker community. One was a young boy named Jacob. Shaker Jacob was now eight years of age. His one living parent, a Shaker sister had converted when he was just an infant. His father's whereabouts was not discussed or known. He had a round face with wondering eyes. He was wistful at times, if that was the word. His brown hair was cut short in a bowl shape. It was the haircut many of the Shaker men or boys wore. He seemed smart and was told of this fact often. He could recite scripture and he liked the outdoors. Winter was a magical time for him, unlike the other children who seemed to thrive as spring and summer arrived. He liked the *jack frost* cold of outdoors and he would take walks treading across the icy branches and leaves that covered the Shaker grounds. He always seemed to be in search of something or someone. Was it his father? It was stated as so, by one of the Shaker brothers. But there was a father he had found; the one who was father in heaven and healed all broken hearts.

V

Labors

How could an object create stillness? And yet it seemed possible with the things the Shakers made; simple furniture and architecture of perfect symmetry, boxes in oval shapes neatly lidded and seeds that seemed superior in texture and appearance. There was an extension of the spiritual in what they created, that was beyond words and recognized as such.

The New Lebanon Shaker Village was American industry at its best and at its most active, it was a magnificent thing. With its' hundreds of buildings spread across a large acreage of land in the Appalachian valley of New York State, it was a sight to see when its Shaker residents and workers were caught up in their separate or collective tasks. Everything was done with a good effort, with care and precision, with a focus on the replication or combined result. Work was a serious matter, God's work, but it could be done with good humor and certainly done with a measure of brotherly or sisterly love. Irrigated water brought crops to life, brooms and boxes and chairs were assembled and finished. The details of a perfectly made chest of drawers re-measured and adjusted as needed. Disputes arose and were settled. Differing opinions were not uncommon and a balanced result found. If ever the Shaker phrase, *Hands to Work and Hearts to God* could be seen in daily living it was at the Shaker village. As American a place as a white-washed fence, or a boat on a river, or a billboard advertising goods, or a dance at the local community hall. But the Shakers had their own kind of dance, one that involved the clapping of hands and the singing of hymns. It was the same kind of ordered movement you might see during the day at the Shaker village but this dancing and praising was of the spiritual kind and was infused with gladness. All was to praise the lord their maker.

It was now a Thursday of that week. There was advance that day in all things as all Shaker hands and hired workers were hard at work at some project or another. It was a day of good weather, and although the colder weather of winter, it was sunny and well above a freezing temperature. A warm coat jacket, and a wool cap and scarf would keep you in comfort. There was harmony in the work and a sense of pride that was tacit but evident in the care and thought that went into all duties. It was God's work and there could only be celebration in this if assigned to human souls.

That day Cyryl looked out at the field and in the distance, he saw his friend Stephen standing there. He never looked more natural in a setting. He was a man who never wanted to be without love or friendship; an ordinary human soul in all possible ways. He looked up at Cyryl and stopped his task; smiled and then waved. He brushed the blond hair away from his forehead with the sleeve of his shirt and then went back to his task without looking up again. The sun in the sky brightened and then faded back behind the haze of clouds. Cyryl marked that day on a paper calendar he kept with his things. It seemed to signify a turning point in his life and he wanted to remember the day.

The mechanisms of machinery, the use of tools and the work of hands created the daily movements of the community. Shaker-owned wagons rolled across the acres of land in the process of some task. The movement of the clouds above in the sky mirrored the slow but steady daily progress below.

Here in this religious community the passing of time, of time itself, seemed more discernible. It represented in the void, the space and the shadow of light. The dimensional representing time pressed as memory and the future as a prophecy found in the abstract. Or the ordinary and familiar images that should not be so, except for their extrasensory symbolism. These being a shadow shape, a texture in dimming light; a Shaker sister or brother nonexistent. The unseen in a drawer or in the corner of a room. And so, time seemed magnified and it was held in the objects that the Shakers made, grew or bespoke.

The work at the Shaker village was hard and the days consumed by it, yet the Shaker brothers and sisters always found time for meetings of prayer, song and dance. They would not have been Shakers without this important spiritual connection.

"I thought the singing and dancing at our last meeting to be lively in spirit," said a Shaker sister.

"Yes, it was a worshipful prayer meeting. In addition to this, I felt it was a good discussion that we had with our Shaker brothers at our community meeting last Wednesday. We have a clearer direction now. I feel we will be led to new prosperity in faith," said another Shaker sister.

"I am looking forward to our brother's and sister's correspondence from Sabbath Day Lake. They are to send a report on their progress with things and future goals, as set out by their conference of members," said Shaker Sister Emily.

"We have completed many of these boxes with many more to finish," said a Shaker sister. She had completed filling a Shaker seed box and had placed it on top of a stack of these.

The Shaker sisters were selecting seeds by hand and putting them into Shaker seed boxes that would be sold at stores throughout New England. Large quantities of these vegetable seeds, in circular Shaker wood boxes, varnished green, yellow and red, sat on a table. These seeds were weighed with a scale and then placed into rectangular wood boxes with dividers, to be delivered to stores to sell. The retail seed boxes had paper labels with the script, *Shaker Choice Vegetable Seeds,* and *Shaker Seed CO. Mount Lebanon, N.Y.* Each seed type in each divided section was identified. These seeds would grow celery, cabbage, turnips, peas and onions. Colorful artwork renderings showed these vegetables in full maturity, fresh from the garden.

A central part of the Shaker community's purpose was the preparation of the lord's return to earth and the final separation of good and evil. The idea of good might be expressed in something beautiful and well-made. Goodness is found inside a drawer of a Shaker dresser, hidden inside a Shaker oval box or found in the fine grain surface of a Shaker table top. Evil can hide inside the framework of a thing; distinguished in its' potential to destroy good. This is vacant in the Shaker object. What one might see is the silent travail of a Shaker; their fervent spiritual devotion as a creative element.

79

The crops had long been harvested and had kept the hired workers and Shaker brothers and sisters busy in the fields and kitchen. But as well as the gathering of seasonal bounty of fruit, herbs and vegetables, many other tasks and industries were attended to. There was the making of chairs and fabric tape for its seating, various other furniture, oval boxes for storage, medicines, braided rugs and woven cloth. The distilling of fine liquor and the irrigation of crops was a daily matter. The weather altered daily activity as a stormy day could stop work in the fields or quickly bring in freshly-laundered clothing put out to dry. A rainstorm was a blessing and yet, so was a bright sunny day. Wind brought movement and sounds, of rustled leaves and other odd noises. Hail, the salt of heaven brought leaves down by the basket-full; fertilizer for future gardens. A dry, dusty day could represent a day for work indoors, such as wood working or the details of building, or it could be the ideal day for outdoor projects like the gathering of hay in the fields or the shucking of corn. But all these days of varied weather and light were gifts from God, to be used to the fullest in the majesty of the lord.

Shaker Brother Ellis had the task of making oval boxes. He had made hundreds of these, all of them completed with the aid of an oval mold. The sides were made of maple wood and the tops and bottoms of pine; clinch nails were used. In all five sizes from smallest to largest, the boxes measured: 2 by 6.5 by 4.5-inches, 2.75 by 8 by 5.5-inches, 3.5 by 9 by 6.5-inches, 4 by 10.25 by 7.25-inches and 4.25 by 11.5 by 8.5-inches. That day, Shaker Brother Ellis was making only one size, the largest of the stack. The finished boxes were now stacked neatly against one wall of the room where he worked. These oval boxes were sometimes varnished with a shade of red, a Shaker blue or a yellow ochre.

A Shaker sister made most of the Shaker chairs at Mount Lebanon. These ladder back chairs had the same colonial influences and style of similar non-Shaker chairs so common in the New England States of America. But the Shakers seemed to refine and simplify their furniture pieces. Shaker furniture was plain looking. Yet, it had a style and beauty all its' own. Its' usefulness told a story, about the maker and the purpose of the piece.

Shaker-made chairs were so well-liked for their quality and style that by the 1870s, many imitators began making copies of these chairs and even referred to them as "Shaker." One of these American furniture companies was the L & G Stickley Company that would later be best known for their oak mission-style furniture pieces. As of result of these imitations, the Shakers of Mount Lebanon, New York began to stamp their Shaker made chairs with a trade mark transfer that identified them as such. These were gold decals made by Palm, Fechteler and Company of Chicago and New York. The chairs trademark reading, SHAKER'S, MT. LEBANON, N.Y.

There was an aura to a Shaker chair that could not be imitated or fully described. It transcended the wood used and praised it as the same time. A fine and useful chair of the highest quality.

In one of the family houses, neatly ironed and folded laundry hung from a wooden frame in the Shaker ironing room. A sister's dress and kerchief hung from two pegs of a wood coat rail fastened to the wall. It floated there like an angel with its sleeves and skirt lifeless, as if the spirit had descended to heaven. The heat from a wood-burning stove in this room made it the warmest in the house. When it was very cold outside, the windows of the room fogged over with condensation. In this room, several Shaker sisters were ironing garments on large tables. Two young girls helped with the folding of laundry and the carrying of the re-heated irons from the hot stove, something they did ever-so-carefully.

Physical fatigue can often be the result of hard work. But there is a spiritual fatigue as well and it can leave a person with very little emotional energy. The will to do ordinary things seems to not be attainable when in this state of mind. But the physical and spiritual go hand in hand and without prayer the daily tasks of life would not be possible. With the knowledge of this, the Shaker prayed for their community, their country America and above all things, guidance from their savior, the lord.

Another day had begun and outdoors, Cyryl and was on his way to work. The wind pushed him back as he walked to the stone barn. Here he was to help with some task. He had not been told what the task would be. As he walked on, again, the wind like an unseen force pushed him back and made the locks of his black hair blow backwards as if smoothing them around his face. The wind along the coast often brought the smell of the ocean or the possibility of rain. It could be hot or cool and full of moisture. The wind he felt that day was of the earth. It brought the smell of it and the leaves on trees. It whipped at his clothes. It made the grass in the yard move about as if a green fabric that had come to life. It opposed him and it was his companion as well, like a Shaker from the past joining him in his assigned activity. Then it was gone as suddenly as it had appeared. Ahead of him was the stone barn, imposing in its structure.

Cyryl was given the task of shucking harvested corn for feed. This corn would be stored in a barn. The bare husks would be used as kindling. The animals needed to be fed daily and at specific times.

There were others who had been taken in for the colder months. Some of these men seemed more reliable than others. Cyryl had stayed close to his friend Stephen and his new friends Bill and Ned. They had gotten to know some of the Shakers. They had done tasks for these Shakers. There was Shaker Sister Fern, who was in charge of a family kitchen and Shaker Brother Gerard who assisted the sisters with their gardens. Shaker Brother Gerard was the eldest of the Shaker brothers and now in his eighties. He was in good health, though, and still a steady worker. He loved telling stories and recalling his Shaker past and he had a fondness for plants and trees.

Cyryl worked alongside Bill that following day. The work was hard. The two were told to unload lumber from a wagon. Lumber to be used for the making of Shaker furniture and chairs. Bill was clearly stronger than Cyryl and could unload the lumber planks without any stress of limb. Cyryl tried to keep up but he faltered under the weight of the long lumber planks and he had to take a few short rests during the unloading. It wasn't that the task had to be done quickly.

It was with Bill's great strength, that it would be accomplished. The unloading of the wood was a job simply needing to be done. And it got Cyryl thinking about the many hard tasks that he might face as a farmer.

"Bill, you said your family owns a farm?" asked Cyryl.

"Yes, but it's too much trouble and the only thing worth a damn is the land and we can't sell it," said Bill.

"I suppose a farm is a lot of work," said Cyryl.

Bill lifted a larger flat plank of wood and threw it neatly on the pile now rising in a corner of the large workroom. It landed with a loud wood-against-wood thud. Dust rose into the air and caught the reflection of sunlight coming from a window.

"It sure is a lot of work; hard work from sun up till sunset," said Bill.

"I am going to farm I think. I might try to find a job in a small town though. A mill might hire me," said Cyryl, still hopeful for work in a mill or factory.

"Why in the heck would you work in a mill?" asked Stephen.

"You think this is hard work?! The heat in the mill can kill a man. Your idea of farming is a better one. You should stay here awhile and learn from these Shakers. They know everything about farming and industry. They're smart and everything they make or sell is of the best quality. They are highly respected people. No one can make furniture like the Shakers. And they make the best liquor you ever tasted," said Bill.

Cyryl's legs sank under the weight of the lumber the two men now lifted from the back of the wagon. The job would be finished within the hour and Cyryl hoped for an easier task to finish out the day. But there was more wood to be moved and unloaded. These were smaller pieces that had to be stacked in a workroom. By the end of the day, Cyryl was exhausted. He had not made any more money than usual. He had certainly earned his wages. His food never tasted so good back at the men's residence. The place looked dingy compared to the Shaker rooms he had seen. He was sitting at the table with the other men. His hands ached and he looked at the redness of his palms. They were as dry as corn husks. He had seen his cloudy reflection in a mercury mirror. His color had darkened from work in the sun. His black curly hair would have to be cut. He had already planned the day; a day to rest and clean himself up. He wanted to look like a gentleman, desirable and dashing like the men in the newspapers and photo reels he had seen. Their hair slicked back and wearing white collar shirts from Paris. That was what he had seen in his red calloused hands and he used them to finish eating his bread in pieces.

Cyryl thought of his parents. Of the one photograph of them as a young couple. They sat next to one another looking dignified. They looked more pleased than smiling. Cyryl marveled at their easy romance. He had never found anything like it. Love had never come to him in that way. Blessed by the blessed virgin, sanctified by God and legalized in the Catholic church. His was more in the form of lust or fleeting love. He was certainly a sinner in the eyes of God. He had forgotten Christ's sacrifice. His sinful life left for a confession that was never made. Was it this new land of America that had left him so restless as a young man? He was more like his father than not, but in the way he was different made him of another generation. His father was more Greek than American. He was American first and Greek.

Natural resources, the bounty of a harvest, human strength and a divine spiritual guidance were what the Shakers used to create their profits. The Shaker men and women usually worked at their daily tasks separately. This separation of men and women seemed natural in some ways and yet unnatural in other ways.

Often, the days Cyryl spent working alongside the Shaker men seemed the best possible way of accomplishing the many tasks that needed to be done. Many of the tasks they knew well and could instruct a workman as to how to complete it. There was a male bond and respect between the men. They enjoyed each other's company and when a disagreement did ensue, it was resolved swiftly and politely.

The Shaker women seemed to enjoy working with a collective energy on a variety of tasks. These included sewing, laundry, cooking and daily cleaning.

"There is no dirt in heaven," Mother Ann Lee had once told a sister as she scrubbed a floor. This quote had often been repeated and contemplated. Gardening, the collection of food, herbs, the making of medicines, canned goods to be sold. These tasks were assigned to the Shaker sisters. But the separation from men was of the ultimate kind as well. There would be no marriage between these Shaker men and women. Kind words and affection expressed certainly, but an important part of the Shaker society life included a vow of celibacy. To Cyryl, it seemed unimaginable. He was the most sexual animal he knew but he would not have dared admit it to a Shaker. This was the unnatural part of this utopian place. It was one of many reasons why he could never be a Shaker.

He was a Catholic at heart and now realized it. He could still see his mother's face as she prayed at church, the prayer beads she held in her worn, thin hands and the tears she sometimes shed for a saint or for what appeared to Cyryl, her own silent human suffering. He had desperately needed work and a new start. He needed shelter for the winter. In his mind, God or Jesus Christ or some divine guidance like the soul of his mother or a remembered relative had led him to these people. He recognized his own romantic thoughts. He was a Greek man. That complicated things a bit for him. He could not live without passion. Passion was a part of life and perhaps the most important part of life. It was then that he knew he would have to move on at some point soon to his own piece of land; to his own life. He would learn what he could from these people. They were kind and God-fearing. The Shakers knew things common to the earth. They knew piety and self-sacrifice, devotion and discipline of mind and heart. But it was God that knew all things. It was God who had planted the tree of life. And their lord and savior guided them through all seasons.

When Cyryl and Shaker Sister Rebecca had first met. It simply happened without any reason or timing. When they had met it had been close to the end of a workday. Cyryl and a group of the other workmen were to complete a task for the Shaker sisters. Cyryl looked a mess with his clothes covered in soot and dirt in his hair. He didn't realize it until later, but his face was smudged with dirt as well and it made him look like a child.

Shaker Sister Rebecca came to the door of the Shaker family house and gave the orders for the men. She was allowed this proximity. The men stood silently as she spoke but they slightly resented a woman so freely telling them what to do. Shaker Sister Rebecca was young and pretty and they were a bit amazed by her presence. So was Cyryl, and when he seemed to catch Shaker Sister Rebecca's attention, he nodded like a gentleman to her. She gave him a sweet but restrained smile. He could only have described it as strict pleasantness. But it revealed much

85

about Shaker Sister Rebecca's character, so much that it was at that moment that Cyryl knew that another young woman hid behind that Shaker uniform. She was sincere, there was no doubt but it was a strict posture that she projected as if she were still trying it on for size. It might have been her youth. She had also been taught that a Shaker woman was equal in all things to a Shaker man. She was to show her good sense and usefulness, her ability to make decisions and lead. She was inside the building now. Shaker Sister Rebecca certainly was pretty. He imagined the two of them setting off and going west in search of a small homestead where they could settle and have a family. He had never acted on such a dream. He had only to make it possible but he didn't want to frighten her off. He must be careful, he thought, in his actions or risk losing his work at the community. His friend Stephen would tell him he was foolish. He would say nothing to the other men who had now left for the workman residence.

The conversation in the workman residence that evening surrounded the contents of a newspaper, this being the New Lebanon, New York's publication.

"These politicians are as dishonest as any carpetbagger!" said Ned. He was referring to an article on politicians running for elected office and the promises they each had made.

"They are carpetbaggers selling promises to the public," said Cyryl.

"This country is still torn apart from the war. I don't think many of the people in the South felt they ever had a say in all of it. Those farmers down there say they won't ever forgive the North. My uncle is one of them in South Carolina," said Bill.

"There's a country western show traveling around the nation. It sounds pretty entertaining. It has real cowboys, buffalo and Indians," said a workman looking over a page of the newspaper.

"That sounds like some fun," said Ned.

It was now near Christmas time. The same electricity was in the air in the Shaker Village as was in the small town of New Lebanon, New York. The festive Christmas decorations inside the homes and in the windows of the New Lebanon storefronts was lacking in the Shaker family houses. But pine boughs and springs of red and green holly branches decorated the Shaker tables and windows of some of the rooms.

On Christmas day, a special dinner would be served. A spice cake was made along with stewed apples with cinnamon. Several fruit pies were also to be served. That year, scripture that told of the lord's birth was read on the eve of Christmas. Snow was on the ground. On Christmas morning, the sun appeared in the sky from behind a cloud cover, bringing sunshine to the land below. It warmed the snow-covered land and made all things bright and radiant. Christmas day labors were kept to a minimum. Youth had become a memory for many of these Shakers but in their hearts, were the youth of all celebrations and seasonal days. There was a sleigh ride and music was performed on instruments. On this Christmas day, there were thoughts of the past, present and the future. The landscape, white and silent, lay before you through a window view as if time had stopped; as a background to the activity of life indoors and far away in the imagination of all men and women. It was a day of celebration everywhere and the idea of it presented itself without sight or sound. *At the time of Christmas, we are more mindful of the fact that we have loved and that the possibility of love and friendship is still there if we wish to find it. With hope in our hearts, we can celebrate the possibility of "peace and good will toward men." It is so at Christmas; a miracle to wonder upon.*

The candles in the Shaker houses seemed to burn more brightly that evening and the star of Bethlehem shown bright in the night sky that was a dark blue. The same star-light that shined down onto the snow and ice-covered ground and the tree-covered Appalachian hills.

The hills looked blue that following morning against the snow-covered fields. Birds flew from the trees, noisy squirrels busied themselves in their branches and the sight a deer running along the edge of the woods reminded one of the abundance of life that thrived in this scenic place. Work commenced at the Shaker community and that day's conversation, in part, was speculation of what the New Year would bring to America and the workers themselves. That conversation was filled with hope and fanciful aspirations but also a dose of realistic assumption. These men that worked the tasks that brought them close to the earth in various ways, knew that there was satisfaction in the simple accomplishments attainable to most worthy and steady men. Winter solstice was in the air like a mist of snow that covered the already snow-covered banks of indefinable land.

There were days when acts of kindness were the only words expressed here. In the completion of a labor that was a response of strength and love. Or a necessity provided, that was not so ordinary on a day. Sometimes noticed by others or only for God's watchful eyes. It was what was at the core of this community of the faithful. Revealed in those Shaker things of usefulness and wholesome human consumption.

Within this time of the later nineteenth century, the Mount Lebanon Shakers were now widely admired for their industry and fine quality products. Approval of their faith was another matter entirely. And so, each trip to a town was done so with confidence and with a measure of caution.

It was a frigid winter morning in New Lebanon, New York. Without a mercury thermometer, the Shaker brothers were unsure of the exact temperature. The crunching sound of snow was heard underfoot as the brothers unloaded their wagon filled with Shaker goods. The early morning sunlight on the red brick buildings made them look yellow and illuminated. The same yellow sunlight was cast onto the snow-covered ground creating gray shadows. Snow edged the buildings roofs and trimmed the window sills. The strong cold wind blew snow flake crystals into the brother's faces. They were thankful for warm coats and woolen gloves. It was one of those crisp, cold and clear winter mornings you would remember your whole life. The townspeople of New Lebanon were dressed for winter weather with coats, knitted wool scarves and warm hats. There were those who dressed more prosperously but most of the town's people wore down-to-earth, practical clothes. It could be said that the society of this small town looked pretty much on the same economic level. They were now quite familiar with the Shakers as their neighbors and many respected them for their industry and fine quality goods. But others saw them as unwelcome competitors and spiritual oddities with their anti-family and communal way of life. With their transactions complete, the Shaker's horse and wagon trotted past the red-brick storefronts which contained the post office and bank, then past a row of poor-looking clapboard houses with a sun scorched white wash.

There was a freshly-painted white wood church with a steeple and then the last house before one left town for the countryside. This a proper Victorian house with a few farm buildings.

The Shaker brothers then traveled to the home of a shop keeper in Stuyvesant town. The travel distance between Mount Lebanon and Stuyvesant town was approximately twenty-seven miles, approximately a three-hour trip by horse and carriage. This is where it was agreed, according to a letter of correspondence, that the Shaker goods would be shown and decided upon as merchandise to sell. The shop keeper's house was built of a smooth limestone and was in a severe classical revival style. A snow from the night before edged the dark windows and roof of the structure. A tall black-iron fence around the front yard made it look an unwelcoming place. The inside of the house held dark, curtained rooms with upholstered furniture. On the walls hung American and European landscape paintings rendered in dark greens and pale blues. The shop keeper, a short, stout man with slicked-down hair greeted the Shaker brothers in a respectful way but wanted a bargain on all items. He softened finally after realizing the Shaker brothers did not deal in this manner and stood firm on the price of their goods, no matter the quantity. But once the transaction had been completed, the Shaker brothers seemed anxious to be on their way.

"He was a most discontented man," said Shaker Brother Matthew. The other Shaker brother nodded in agreement.

"We should pray for him," said Shaker Brother Matthew.

After this first transaction, other errands were made in town. Then the trip back was made to the Mount Lebanon Shaker community against a wind that fiercely swept the land snow up in great flurries against the carriage and horses as it followed the country road.

And so, the first of the winter months seemed to pass quickly and there was always plenty of work to do in the large Shaker Village. The workmen, including Cyryl and Stephen were content in their lodging and what was provided to them. It was very hard work and the leisure time they had was often spent resting and keeping warm from the winter elements of Northern New York.

VI

The Blizzard

———————————

That morning was cold and crisp with snow in the air. Then the snow came in great flurries. The wind had grown strong and gusting. The top branches of the bare trees shook against the gray sky. It would be a blizzard by the looks of it. Shaker sisters and brothers hurried about in the blowing white of the storm. Their voices barely heard over the sound of it. Soon the landscape was covered in white. The tree branches half-covered with it. Fence posts had conical peaks. Once familiar things in the village yards were now mounds of snow. Most outdoor work came to an end early that day. The snow had forced the Shakers indoors. They had to obey God's law of nature. The snow continued to accumulate and the question of completing the most important labors arose. They had never seen a snow storm like this one. It would bar the doors of buildings and the doors to the animals that needed feeding. The roofs were strong and the hay and crops would stay dry. But it now became evident that whatever tasks needed to be done, had to be done as quickly as possible.

Cyryl had been working alone in a Shaker building of purpose and a distance from the workmen's dwelling. He knew he needed to head back. He had been caught in the beginning of the fierce snow storm. As he went against the wind and blowing snow, he seemed to lose his direction. To Cyryl, it was the same as a terrible storm at sea, but now on land. It was not the bell on a ship that rang out in warning but the unheard bell in the Shaker community that gathered its' faithful members and hired workers to action. He had not seen a snow fall like this one.

During the night before, the March rain had mixed with snow and the wind had increased in its' force. That next morning the appearance of a snow storm shown itself in surprising fury.

It was these strong climactic elements that gave rise to a curiosity in Cyryl as he crossed an open field adjacent to the tilled land and buildings

90

of Shaker purpose. He walked against the increasing wind and blowing snow and listened to the sound of it. He wondered about the combined atmospheric conditions that would bring about such a terrible storm. How long he had walked he was not sure. There were stretches of light in the sky like a luminous aurora. But most of it was dark and opaque in its' colorless limit. He now seemed lost. He was not sure of his own course.

His lone figure trudged forward in the snow storm. What was before him he could no longer see and fear caught his soul. The wind-blown snow erased any perspective view of land. The sky was still visible above him but a blank eerie gray illumination. He thought of a compass and the use of it. He knew that he should be headed East but had he veered too far in another direction to end up lost in this dangerous storm? He was not sure.

He quickened his pace. Yes, it seemed he was on the sea again, battling against a fierce sea storm. Great waves appeared around him; the surface of the ocean turbulent and full of sea spray It was a sea far from land. A shimmering light on its dark waters reflecting the past and too, the future. This storm had raged for many days. The nights were cold and dark; the daylight gray. The forceful wind threw him back and the snow it carried, wet and cold, covered his face with the same salty taste as a bitter sea spray. Terrible crashing sea waves now appeared before him. This place that was once calm and deep blue, was now sea foam and filled the angry rath of something immeasurable in size and rage.

The sea could be a woman or a man. When it was a man, it somehow seemed more compassionate to him. Being a man, he too felt the deep feelings of all men. It cried for all sailors and fishermen. Man belonged on land. But for some unanswered question, these men preferred the sea.

The sea as a man was calling out to him at that moment. He appeared in the sky. He was Dutch, a Greek and yet, he was French and part Mediterranean Spanish. He was Neptune, Roman king of the sea, Pan, Greek patron god of fishing. Palaemon, a Greek sea god who aided sailors in distress. It was Ahti, Finnish god of the depths and fish; the Norse and Germanic Njord, god of the sea. He was even a part of Christ the savior, in his terrible suffering. Cyril almost lost his balance as he trudged forward through the storm.

91

It was a great, white snow-hurricane before him. The changing sky now with a sunlight filtered through clouds. In this wintry force were the transforming elements that made ordinary things seem particles of mystery. Blurring the familiar to something foreign and unseen. He looked up at the sky and swirling snow. His vision of the sea was gone.

He paced on and at last, there seen before him was the light from the Shaker building's windows. He had gone in the right direction after all. He hurried to get back to his safe dwelling place and a meal.

Once safely indoors, Cyryl hung up his wet coat and cap and went to look for his friend Stephen and found him in his bed sleeping. His blond hair had grown long was curled around his ears and neck. He lay there looking like a young boy; angelic and quiet. Alas, he would tell him of his snow adventure at meal time.

"Cyryl, what's the matter?" asked Stephen, having suddenly awakened and seeing Cyryl looking at him.

"I got caught in the snow storm," said Cyryl.

"I wondered where you might be. I must have fallen asleep," said Stephen.

"Have you looked outside at the snow? It is a real blizzard. We are indoors for the day I would think," said Cyryl.

"They will want us to clear paths in the snow once it stops," said Stephen. "Animals have to be feed. Work on a farm doesn't stop because of a snow storm."

Now indoors for a time Cyryl began to think about his time at the Shaker village and what he and Stephen had experienced. It had been a great deal of hard work and learning. He saw it as a good thing and he felt they had found providence in their new circumstances, however brief they might be. He had never experienced the seasons like this. How different it was living in the city. How different it had been working on the sea.

The great storm did not subside. And the snow continued to fall that night and the following day. The snow storm seemed endless in its' capacity. It would create snow drifts of the greatest height any Shaker or other local peoples had ever seen. It was an event of nature they would always remember; marking their history and that of the state and area with the recollection of it. As recorded in the month of March in that eighty-eighth year, of that nineteenth century.

The great amount of snow had made invisible the New Lebanon and Lebanon Springs Roads. Both buried beneath several feet of it. These narrow dirt roads once seen between a slight hillside and the proper land of the Shaker buildings. Now all before them was an endless white landscape with only an unfamiliar variation of surface. It was an extraordinary transformation, holding all things in place as if frozen in time. And only by another act of nature would it be sufficiently resolved. It was to be a long and late winter; historic in measure and unusual in its' extremes.

The Mount Lebanon Shaker Village had been brought to a standstill. The Shaker brothers and workmen had shoveled a narrow path in the snow to the barn to feed the animals and do the milking. Outdoors, the wind chill made it seem frigid. Smoke from the chimney of the house billowed against a sky that showed only patches of blue but enough to bring some sunshine. How foreign and altered the landscape looked. The Shaker sisters would stay indoors. There was plenty to do. As a topic of discussion, it was one of the strongest snow storms they could remember. There was knowledge to be learned from the past for the future. They surmised on this and other topics.

It was the following day and now only slight flurries of snow fell from the sky. Sunlit shades were cast from the old trees onto the snow-covered land. Ice hung from their branches. The altered shape of the land was made of tall increases and swirling allusions of snow. It was a strange site of crooked land levels and reduced structures. Of anxious sky and grayish-blue clouds.

Window sills and rooftops now billowed in snow arcs. Profound shapes had risen from nowhere; unrecognizable curves of things gave hidden elements a new dimension and depth. Sand-dune shapes of snow had appeared alongside a fence. The trees in the yards were dusted white.

The Shaker brothers and the workmen went outdoors having removed the snow from the entryways to dwellings. But not without some difficulty in getting the doors open against the drifted snow. The landscape before them was one they had not seen before. The ordinary form of all things expanded in height and overstated in extent. Always true to an original structure and yet peaked to an affect unrecognized and even strange. Ordinary shadows seemed cast aside as if untrue to the things they echoed. No longer exact in their reflective darkness. The heavy ice that had formed on branch twigs and shrubs made them silver and reflective in the winter sunlight. Fashioning them into complex ice shapes and connecting them to vertical icicles and snow.

The extended valley and hills had been cloaked by the deep snow. The outlines and shapes of it making the distant land a thing of wonder. The wind would modify its' shape and at random, expose the height of things. The sunlight making great blue shades across its' surface of white.

"Let's clear this snow from all needed paths, said a Shaker brother. Let's follow the path of footprints made this early morning to the barn."

The branches of the pine trees covering the Appalachian hills still held the heavy snowfall of the snow storm. More snow fell that day. The sky was illuminated as its' edge above the trees and along the horizon. The cold air turned chimney smoke to a mist. The frozen snow crust made a crunching sound under boots and shoes. The wonder of orange and red fall leaves seen in it.

The next day seemed full of magic. It was a day of severe light and shadow and the distortion of color. The sight of a Shaker brother or sister could be seen and then the figure gone, as if only a memory or shadow. Activity was slow or quick. Slow if one was walking uphill or quick if descending a wet and icy one. Workmen waved their arms to one another in the process of completing a chore. Most of these assigned labors related to the removal of snow or a plan of overcoming it. Cyryl would soon be outdoors helping as well. He thought of his getting lost in the storm. He then went to have his breakfast.

That evening Indian spirits made themselves known at the Shaker prayer meeting. The winter wind shook the tree branches outside, casting their shadows onto the walls of the meeting room until the window shutters were closed by a brother.

A Shaker brother surmised.

"It is winter and the land appears white and with the gray coloring of the season. Yet, if you look closely, within this winter landscape there is a glint of light, a tiny prism of separated colors; the origin of which is white, pure and radiant and made by God's hand."

The changing Appalachian seasons were always there as a background to day and night. You prayed for abundance and triumph of good over evil. The two seeming obvious in their separation of divine light. The human spirit would always rise above fatigue and sorrow with the lord's guidance and blessing. Prayer and celebration in dance and song would be the pathways.

On that day, the workmen were sketches against the bright sunlit snow landscape. They were young men and you knew this, even seeing them at a distance. The caps and hats on their heads, and the coats that they wore, did not disguise this fact but made them look jaunty and youthful. They had strength and energy and they were quick in their forceful movements.

The shorter winter days ended with an early night. The sky as if it had never fully awakened. All things seen in the dim light of this season. An unseen sunlight allowed for a day's hard work. The passing of the hours like the turning of a clock's hands. Then at day's end, the candle was relit and the wood-burning stove rekindled.

There was an image unseen within the Appalachian landscape, held by the haze of snow moisture and the shifting light and shadows of winter. Often in the winter months, whether it was day or night, the ice-crusted top of the snow-covered ground captured the sun or moonlight above; luminous pale blue, white or gray shadow. That morning the sunlight was a queer hue that made the snow-covered ground a darker shade of blue. Smoke rose from the chimneys of the building's where there was human activity. There was much activity that day, but now the day had ended and it was almost time for sleep. Candle and lamp light could be seen in windows of the Shaker family houses. Smoke still rose from the chimneys and was now mixed with the dim stars in the night sky. The weather was harsh and snowy. A wind intermittently blew the snow off the tops of snow drifts and seemed to move along the surface of the land in an airy dance. It was typical of an Upstate New York blustery winter night.

The following day should have been ordinary but it was not. It was full of emotion and drama. Evening prayers asked for a release from satan's power to frustrate and upend.

Shaker Sister Rebecca had finished all that she was to do that day. All that was left were her devotions. She sat with bible in hands in a sitting room, now alone as the other sisters had gone to bed. She had requested to stay in this room for a brief time to reflect and pray. She knew she had been adopted by the Shakers. It had been told to her as a young child. This told her in the most loving way and she loved her adopted Shaker family. The Shaker village had always been her home. But that evening was the first in her life that she had felt separate from them. What would her life have been if her parents were still living? It wasn't the first time she had thought of it. She would surely not have been a Shaker sister. Never had she felt so lost inside. The handsome Greek workman had done this to her. He wished to mock her in some way. He was foolish and uneducated. He had spoken crudely to her? But he had not. He was a man who was not used to Shaker ways. He would display his attraction to a woman as he always had. She would be kind to him but keep her distance. He had nowhere to go for the winter and most probably he would leave in the spring like most of those who stayed for a winter. He had made her think of herself as a woman in a completely different way. She had imagined herself as a mother and wife. The children of the Shaker school classroom had become her own. Something had stirred inside of her. A desire she had not known before. She looked down at the bible that was in her hands. It had always comforted her during those times when her heart was filled with despair and loneliness. A passage from the bible would bring her peace of heart and she recited scripture from it to herself before going upstairs to her bed.

She had never felt such loneliness as she did this night. As she climbed the stair, her slow-moving shadow cast by the candle in her hand against the wall looked like a symbol of her very soul. A ghostly spirit seemed to be present in the hallway. It was that combination of quiet, shadow and light, daylight or an evening candle light, that caused you to pause and left you with a feeling of not being alone. Usually, it was the presence of a spiritual energy that seemed a part of the past in memory; pressed onto the space as if a record of time. It could be discontented;

unsettled as if trying to catch your attention. To tell you of some unspoken thought or regret. Shaker Sister Rebecca acknowledged the spiritual presence and recalled that pray sent away such entities to heaven. This in the hope of their soul finding salvation. Shaker Sister Rebecca said this prayer of amity and then entered the room where she slept.

That evening, Cyryl lay awake in his bed. He felt as if he were waiting for something to happen. There should be important moments in a man's life; birth, marriage, the birth of children, success, tragedy, revenge, failure and death. These things would happen as they should.

One of the workmen had fallen that day. His arm, elbow and his hand was swollen badly. The pain was manageable. The Shakers had brought an Arnica ointment upon hearing of the accident. His arm was bandaged up and he lay in his bed. He had a dinner of soup from a tin cup as a few other workmen brought him pieces of bread and cake to eat. He grumbled at his misfortune.

"I fell down on my right side and hard. I knew it was bad because the swelling started all at once."

"You've got to watch yourself there," said a workman. "That will take some time to heal."

"You get some rest," said another workman.

A sense of civility filled the air. Cyryl had never seen these workmen so compassionate. They weren't all rough talk after all. They could feel for another man's suffering and sympathize with his misfortune. Fishermen were more silent in their responses to their fellow man, as if some higher force shaped the good or bad fortunes of men. If not God, then something outside of themselves that affected their destiny, not unlike an unpredictable sea tide.

Living on land *was* more civilized. Much more than the social interactions of a sailor or a fisherman on a typical day at sea. Life and work on the sea made you forget polity. The individual became foremost. Life nothing more than an act of survival.

VII

The Faithful

The physical result of the Mount Lebanon community reflected religious devotion and great human effort. The Shaker buildings and their interior furnishings were simple and practical. They had a precise symmetry and style.

One building called the Great Stone Barn was built in 1859. There was the Dwelling House with fifty-five rooms. The place where a Shaker went to rest at night was a shared retiring room. In it for each Shaker was a single person bed. In the room might be a side table or a small desk and armless chair with a half-circular, spindle back. A rectangular braided rug usually covered a section of the plank floor of the room. A wooden sconce on the wall held a candle used at night. In this candle-light, the shadows of objects in the room were slanted and magnified. As the candle sputtered near its end, these shadows danced in its' light. The reflected candle-light in the window panes gave a foreshadowing of the future. Although fitted for several Shaker members, this room could seem lonely, but not often, as the exchange of words or a prayer would send such feelings of discomfort away. Life *could* be lonely. It could also be joyous but the mission of the Shaker did not include the emotional comfort of an ordinary human life. It could be the suffering of physical isolation unspoken in the day of Shaker activities. An expression of affection, a simple handshake, a smile or a rare embrace might send it away. Or the childhood memory of a father's or mother's love. The activity of sharing music and dancing could heal that sort of human pain.

It was said by many that the Shakers were a strange people. They had great energy but it was hard to define what kind of energy it was exactly. A mix of religious fervor that seemed to be acted out in dance and sounds and some thought, unorthodox behavior. They spoke in tongues. They shook at times or writhed in spiritual ecstasy.

98

It could not be said that Shakers were supportive of traditional marriage and family values. Love and sexual activity had been divorced. Although it had not fully bloomed, to allow a romantic union between Shaker Sister Rebecca and the workman Cyryl would be viewed as a threat to the community and its' way of life. Above all things, the Shakers knew the fragility of their survival. Of dwindling members and modern-day realities.

The Shakers felt it was a time for a renewal of faith. The winter storm had reminded them of God's power over nature and its elements. He made the seasons. He brought the light and darkness. It was a sign of his great strength and power over the world and mankind. The Shakers would respond with dancing and songs and with the praising of God. The Shakers sang loudly; folk hymns that they had composed and authored. There was clapping of hands and the sound of feet dancing across a plank wood floor. This dancing sound was at times a shuffle and then a marching kind of sound. The Shakers would dance in a circle; women in one direction and the men in another. Gender difference reflected and symbolized by movement in opposite directions; all connected by their belief in Christ. A spiritual connection can be symbolized by a circle. It has neither a beginning nor an end. And so, we find ourselves within that spiritual connection as opposed to entering or leaving it. We are either a part of it or not. Those around us are too, connected to the same experience of spiritual continuity but might have another interpretation of it.

Cyryl could not imagine this type of behavior in a Catholic church; this dancing and clapping of hands. He didn't doubt their faith in Jesus Christ or God. All you had to do was be around them for a short while to see their piety and reverence to God. Cyryl thought them clever and odd. Yes, they were clever at making things and learning for themselves. Their religion he did not fully understand. He was starting to see, though, that it was their very strict ways and separation from the world that made them so productive and thriving; the basis of it religious faith, their self-discipline, truth and hard work.

Daylight filtered through clouds cast a sheen on the surface of the ice-covered snow in the field. This was due to a light rain that had fallen. The now hardened snow surface crunched under the weight of Cyryl's boots as he walked to the stone barn where he was to work that day. It was a good day's work but he missed the conversation of the other men. That day he worked alone and alongside the Shaker brothers, who often remained silent during their many hours of work; unless the talk was of the task.

Another day came after a night of light snowfall. The sky had been pink and yellow that morning along the horizon. Frozen footprints in the snow could be seen, as paths between houses and other buildings. The faint shadows of the buildings were cast onto the snow-covered ground in odd angles.

While standing in front of a door, Shaker Sister Emily dropped the keys she was holding in her hand. It upset her slightly each time the keys landed in a noisy jangle on the ground or floor. This was something she had started to do more and more as she grew elderly. It was a sign of old age. She would sigh and then stoop down and patiently pick them up again. It was a circular metal ring that held many heavy keys. Of course, she would drop them from time to time, but she wished it were less often. She picked them up. The snow-covered keys now felt icy cold to her bare fingers. Shaker Sister Emily was the decision maker among the Shaker sisters. And in this regard, her role was closer to that of the Shaker brothers in certain ways. She had a kind and pleasant face that made you wonder what she might have looked like as a young girl. She had kept her pretty facial features and clear fair skin, although, her face and her hands were now wrinkled in places like an apple from the orchard left to dry in the sun. She was loved by all, as she had a good heart and always seemed to think of others, rather than her own needs. She made sure a birthday cake was made, or a special day acknowledged. She wrote Shaker hymns and she could sew and tailor and bake. She was book-learned and not unknowing of the outside world and of current events. Although, she never discussed these topics outside of a formal meeting of Shaker brothers and sisters. She was a good Shaker member.

Was satan at work that day? That was the thought that Shaker Brother Smith asked himself. A feeling of dread and depression had overcome him that morning. Didn't Christ take away all feelings of hurt and fear? He did, and so he prayed to the lord for comfort. But he knew that the ache in his heart would stay with him and he did not know why. It wasn't something he could easily relate to the other Shaker brothers without appearing to be frail in spirit and faith. At the appropriate time during prayer service that evening, he would speak of it and frame it as a lesson. Yes, a lesson in strength of spirit and the wish to be Christ-like in one's action. Most importantly, in examining the soul and finding strength in daily tasks. But his was a deep sorrow that he could not rationalize away, as if he was accepting the passing of something, or someone unknown and un-named. He longed for and pitied himself for the unidentified loss and the mark it would leave on his heart. Not all things could be shared with other men or women and even the Lord Jesus could only act as a shepherd at times and leave his flock to wander as they might.

It was in the yard that the terrible depression that Shaker Brother Smith had felt the day before, came over him again.

"What is wrong Brother Smith? said a Shaker brother standing closest to him.

"He's not feeling well, said another Shaker brother. "Are ye not feeling well, Brother Smith?"

Shaker Brother Smith stood still and was a bit stooped over. He seemed frozen in his forward pose. He uttered no words or sounds.

"He has gotten too much sun or has simply failed in strength," said a Shaker brother.

This time it seemed too much for him and he was helped from the yard. It was his cry for help to no one that alerted the other brothers that something terribly wrong had happened to Shaker Brother Isaac. A shadow had crossed over the land just as Shaker Brother Smith had fallen ill in spirit. The Shaker brothers had noticed it most certainly. Cyryl also at work outdoors had seen it, and he grew quiet inside of himself. It had been a dramatic moment in nature. An omen, or at the least a symbol of some bad energy within the earth or above it. At least it seemed as such, in this uncommon community where goodness was represented as light and evil as darkness. The separation of it at the center of their faith.

The Shaker brothers were now praying with Shaker Brother Smith. Two of the Shaker sisters saw that the men had gathered about one of the Shaker brothers and had now joined them to inquire as to the matter. Eventually, the ailing Shaker brother was walked to the house where he

101

resided. This was a good place thought Cyryl. But bad things can happen anywhere. Should he pray as well? He thought about it a moment and then made the sign of the cross and looked up at the sky. The large cloud that had passed over the field covered a portion of the sky. Cyryl continued with his work. He thought about the time his father had fallen ill, but he had recovered. He thought about the death of his mother and how he had noticed her hands in those final moments of life. Hands that had cared for him and his siblings. They were hands that had cooked and sewn and cleaned their small rooms on the Lower East Side of New York. They were beautiful hands, aged and worn. His own hands were still strong. He would use them to build something for himself.

It was a night when one could only see a partial view of stars in the cloudy night sky. Rising above the valley land, the Appalachian hills were only an outline of what they had been before sunset. The morning light of sunrise revealed a snow-covered land edged with tree-covered hills and a dark, opaque sky. The weather was unusually cold. Closer to the woods, the branches that had fallen from the trees were on the ground, once attached and thriving. A strong wind had brought them down broken and lifeless. The wind rose and died and the sky above seemed more ominous with its' hazy cloud cover. It seemed as if another season would not arrive after this one. We would always be at the mercy of cold temperatures, a colorless sky and bare tree branches never to return as green-leafed. The weather seemed to represent a lack of knowing. The darkness of ignorance. The limits of want and need.

The only book Cyryl owned was a worn copy of a text by the great Roman orator, Cicero. He had bought it in New York City at a book store and he had kept it with him, for it represented knowledge and superior thoughts. This was: *Offices: Essays on Friendship and Old Age and Selected Letters* by Cicero. Much of it he could not read. Only fragments of sentences were identifiable to him. But what he did comprehend seemed important. "The danger of some actions only related to the person that undertakes them, "(he had been read this part of a sentence by another seaman). "…always think it necessary to exhibit the noble youth,…" He wasn't sure what this meant but it sounded important and he had memorized the page number that (201) it was on. The book represented to him a higher understanding of life that he wished to achieve on some level. He could only understand a few words but he read them and imagined the rest as he usually had done.

He was asked about the book in his hand, by a Shaker brother.

"It is a book by Cicero, the Roman orator," said Cyryl.

"Thou should have a bible to read for idle hours and the Sabbath. I think we can provide a copy of God's word for you. No man's words are greater than God's word. That is vanity and boastfulness. You see the ruin it brought to mankind, in the fall of the evil Roman Empire," said a Shaker brother.

"Cicero was a great man and he spoke well. He taught fairness of law and the importance of truth," said Cyryl.

"That may well be, but there is no greater truth than God's. Keep your book. I will offer you a bible as well. Compare them and tell me what you think," said the Shaker brother.

"If you wish to do this for me, that is fine. I will find the time to read the Bible as well. I wish to know all I can about this world and the afterlife," said Cyryl.

"The afterlife, young Cyryl, is heaven if you wish it, but it may likely be hell if a man's ways are not mended. I will bring you a bible for I fear you are headstrong in your path to the latter," said the Shaker brother.

Brother left the room and Cyryl was left to read his book of Cicero. The Roman Cicero, the great orator! Obviously, these Shakers did not have a wider view of the world. It was a narrow one that was filled with pettiness and prejudice. Had not the Greek Catholics been prosecuted for their faith? Had they not been faithful to Christ's teachings all the same? Good Greek Catholics like his father and mother. He saw now why the Shakers had thrived so well. To them their faith was the correct faith, the only faith and they meant to preserve it. Every board planed and nailed. Every task and labor was God's work, an expression of their Shaker God and his son, Christ Jesus. He had seen religious devotion but not like this. This was a...and he had to think for a moment. A strength born of religious thought and action, and he admired it and he would learn from it. He could never be a Shaker. He was a Catholic, if he was of any

103

religious faith. It was something he would keep to himself. He was a Catholic and he admired Cicero. And if he could learn to read and write better, that would be a benefit as well.

It was now past winter. The fields would soon re-awaken in spring and the ground would turn to muddy earth and new growth. That evening at their worship service The Shakers sang a song that was an expression of religious faith. Their plain and resounding voices heard out-of-doors and apart of the community setting.

It was the birthday of Shaker Brother Matthew and the Shaker sisters had made him a yellow cake with a vanilla frosting. It was brought to the table after the evening meal had been served. Shaker Brother Matthew thanked the sisters and they all had a piece of the cake with a green herbal tea. Shaker Brother Matthew thanked God for bringing him to that day and all the things he had been blessed with. Days on earth were never a certainty and that was the spiritual message Shaker Brother Matthew wished to share.

That evening the Shaker brothers and sisters sat together at a prayer meeting. They all agreed that it had been a good day of accomplishments. They acknowledged that they were more to each other than Shaker brothers and sisters. They were children of god. And it was Christ their father that sat at the head of their table.

The workmen usually kept to themselves with little interaction with the Shaker men but that morning, as it happened, Cyryl was in a conversation with a Shaker brother.

"America is much more beautiful than the way it looks in paintings."

"You know something of art Cyryl?" asked the Shaker brother.

"I went to the Boston Museum of Art once, and I saw a lot of paintings. Many of these were landscapes as they are called. I have seen copies of paintings as well."

"Was there an artist that you liked the most?" asked the Shaker brother.

"I liked the paintings of Mr. John Frederick Kensett. But no painter could show the real beauty of this New York land as it really is today," said Cyryl.

The Shaker brother was quite surprised by Cyryl's knowledge of American painters, enough to have chosen a favorite among them.

"I believe you are probably exact in your consideration. We cannot fully render what God has created. We strive for it in our community of Shaker brothers and sisters. But it is only an earthly representation of heaven. You seem to want to do more with your life. Are you sure you want to be a simple farmer?" asked the Shaker brother.

"I am almost sure. I am not well-learned and my parents, Greek immigrants, were poor. I want to return to New York City someday, but only to visit. My papa is still living there. I did not like living in a city when I was a child. It was noisy and smelled bad. I like the idea of planting things; of growing crops. I may not get rich, but then again, I might have the good fortune of being well-off; a land owner. And there is one other thing I wish for. I had to leave school at an early age to help my family make a living. I want to learn to read and write correctly," said Cyryl.

The secular world outside of the Mount Lebanon Shaker community was dramatically different and greatly influenced by non-spiritual pursuits and modes of living. During this nineteenth- century era, American men wore a variety of styles in hat wear and facial hair styles from clean-shaven to a full-groomed beard. Fashionable women wore button shoes and feathered hats, if they could afford such a frivolous luxury. Hope and the promise of a better future was the theme as it had always been during this young nation's history. In this New England area, both the American cities of New York and Boston greatly influenced the populations around them. Their urban styles of fashion and thinking filtered down to the smaller cities and towns of New York and the rest of the now reunited American States. The Shakers did not isolate themselves to the extent of ignorance regarding current affairs and political thought. Newspapers were available to purchase in nearby New Lebanon, New York and a Shaker brother or sister would read from and discuss with others, the current events described and related to in these publications. The art of conversation was vital to a man and woman of success and influence. It was stimulated daily as part of the day's important activities; personal style and character filtered such communication to an individual manner and progression. Even the laborer or farmer had his approach and routine regarding the exchange of opinion and thought. It had become a part of the American common landscape. To be able to read and write was most necessary if one were to be a part of this social exchange of ideas and personal expression.

In New York, theatrical plays were dramatizing popular culture and events in America and Europe. George Frederick Bristow's *Winter Tale Overture* might be performed at a concert hall. Figures of minor celebrity or politicians that were hated or admired, were discussed around the checker board or on the front stoop of a shop owner's establishment. New inventions that seemed miracles of efficiency and usefulness were created by the ever clever and adapting human. It was during this time that electricity was discovered by Thomas Edison. Mark Twain published *The Adventures of Mark Twain.* A non-alcoholic drink called *Coca-Cola* was introduced to the American consumer. The railroad that now linked the country brought a boom of prosperity and faster news of American and world events. The amazing phonograph and phonograph records were commercially produced for the first time. Yet, with all the hope and new prosperity, ignorance and fear often prevailed. African-Americans newly freed by former President Lincoln's Emancipation Proclamation, were the consistent victims of lynching in the American Southern States. Crime and traveling vagabonds seemed to be more common.

Some part of the American experiment had spoiled and was often depicted in the cartoon editorials of a local newspaper publication. But mostly, it was a time of peace and prosperity resulting in a quickly changing American landscape that grew more populated, diverse and sophisticated. And somehow, along with these great changes, the Shakers and their communities had become as American as any other part of this great human experiment in democracy.

VIII

Lessons

It was cooler out that morning and the night-time rain had been reduced to a light sprinkling. The wind shook cold rain drops from the trees. The shade of the trees seemed darker. The beginning of sunshine crept out from behind the clouds.

Later that morning, Cyryl appeared at the side door of the Shaker house and knocked.

"Is Sister Rebecca in?" asked Cyryl.

A Shaker sister had come to the door looking much surprised.

His heart pounded as he waited for a response. She might not be able to come to the door. He had on a clean suit of clothes. He had shaved and his hair was cut short and combed neatly to one side. Between the narrow lapels of his short, slim-fitted black jacket and barely seen, was the edge of a white collar and a silk necktie. His slacks were a lighter color of gray. His shoes were polished black. He looked very handsome and very Greek. Shaker Sister Rebecca came to the door, examined him for a moment and then almost laughed.

"What a transformation Cyryl! Where are you going to, dressed so nicely?" asked Shaker Sister Rebecca.

Cyryl took off his hat and nodded a greeting in Shaker Sister Rebecca's direction.

"I am going into town for the afternoon. I wanted to ask if you needed anything?" asked Cyryl.

"That is very nice of you," said Shaker Sister Rebecca. She could not think of anything that the sisters needed but she was touched by his desire to assist her. She then decided to make up an errand.

"Could you bring me some sugar perhaps from the general goods store? One pound of sugar for baking?" asked Shaker Sister Rebecca. Sugar was certainly something the sisters could always use.

107

"Yes, I could do that. I have been to the general goods store in New Lebanon before," said Cyryl.

"Wait here and I will write a note for you. We have an account at the store and they will add this to our monthly order," said Shaker Sister Rebecca.

Cyryl had impressed her he thought. When she handed him the note, their eyes met. His were as dark as olives and Shaker Sister Rebecca's a hazel blue. This time her smile was a sweet one, without any severity or reservation. She realized his sincerity to please her. He was the most charming man she had ever seen and the most handsome. She was most certainly in love but she could not allow herself to fully accept the fact. What did she know of romantic love? It was something in books and of the outside world. God had placed her elsewhere. She only observed this romantic feeling with curiosity at first. The full emotional impact of it was yet to come.

Shaker Sister Emily stood outdoors and looked out at the hills surrounding the Shaker village. She had done this before and the others had noticed. But no one had the courage to ask her what she was thinking until one day a Shaker brother her asked that very question.

"What is it that you're thinking about Sister Emily? he asked.

"Well, she said. She had a reflective tone in her voice and her face grew wrinkle lines that formed around her mouth and eyes. I think about my being here. Sometimes I say a prayer but other times I do not. I think of my momma and my papa. I think about what they would think of their daughter as a Shaker," said Shaker Sister Emily.

"What do you think they would have thought?" asked the Shaker brother.

"I think they would have thought it just fine as long as I loved the lord; lived my life for the lord," said Shaker Sister Emily.

"That's a simple Shaker answer," Sister Emily, said the Shaker brother.

"I am sure you are correct to think it so."

Lightening illuminated the sky. The first few sounds of rain were seen in the movement of tree leaves and wet grass.

It had been decided upon, and with the approval of Shaker Sister Emily, that Shaker Brother Isaac would set aside time and teach Cyryl the workman to read. Shaker Sister Emily had a pensive look on her face. She pursed her lips and thought for a moment. If a Shaker brother could find the time to teach Cyryl to improve his reading and writing, she thought it would be a kindness. Cyryl would not likely stay within the Mount Lebanon Shaker Village. He would need to read a letter or even an important document. These were valuable things to a man. It is God's wish. I feel it. And so, it was decided that Cyryl should be taught to read and write as well as time allowed.

And so, these lessons commenced at a building where the Shaker children attended school.

"Read from this book of stories usually used as a lesson book for the young; a sentence or two," said Shaker Brother Isaac.

"Cyryl was silent at this request." He was looking down at the book in his hands. His face held no expression. He read only parts of the sentences before him in the book and with some hesitation. Words and phrases he recognized, but he struggled with some parts of it. He had understood enough to guess its' topic, but his ability was not the usual proficiency of the average adult that had finished middle school.

"I cannot read too much of it, really," said Cyryl, sounding discouraged.

"You did fine, but I think you would profit greatly from some lessons to help your comprehension of words that form common sentences and then practice writing these," said Shaker Brother Isaac.

"I can only read words, sometimes a few words within in a sentence. I am able to understand their meaning," said Cyryl. His heart sank at the memory and admittance of his limited education in the reading and writing of the English language.

"You will improve quickly," said Shaker Brother Isaac. "I will teach you. Now, you said you had been taught to read as a young child but had forgotten much of your lessons, mostly from lack of required reading or writing?" asked the Shaker brother.

"I did attend school at first, at a young age. But I went to work when I was ten. I was forced to leave school and work alongside a man who sold vegetables on the street. This was on the Lower East Side of New

York. I was too young to protest. I had no choice. My father was a fisherman for a time but he had illness and we needed the extra money to live. His heart was not good. My mother took in laundry and she did tasks such as sewing. She was a very good seamstress," said Cyryl.

"So, you read very little then," said Shaker Brother Isaac.

"I am afraid so. I hope you do not think I deceived you," said Cyryl.

"No, no…it is fine Cyryl. I will teach you as I teach my younger pupils at school. There is no shame in learning, only in not trying to learn."

"Let's start with the alphabet and then I will have you write a few simple words," said Shaker Brother Isaac.

Cyryl's lessons went on for several weeks and as it turned out, he began to remember the childhood lessons he had completed in reading and writing. His advancement was quick and Shaker Brother Isaace was greatly impressed with his quick learning.

Yet, it was along with the discovery of words and their meaning that other emotions and thoughts appeared to Cyryl. There was the pain of losing his mother. There was also the acknowledgement of how lonely he had felt at times when living the life of a fisherman. He acknowledged those he had loved and still loved in various ways. He realized that he had his own intellectual curiosity. It wasn't that he hadn't known of his own wish to learn and more specifically to read, but how he had attempted to learn in small abbreviated ways. It said something about his own self as a Greek man and the family of Megalos. They weren't just uneducated rural townsfolk and poor farmers. There was a history there, a genetic memory of something much greater and rich in the knowledge of words and the philosophical understanding of human action.

One evening after supper, Cyryl had a more private conversation with his friend and travel companion, Stephen.

"I miss the sea a little, but being a fisherman or a sailor is a hard living," said Stephen.

"You feel land locked?" asked Cyryl.

"No, I like working on land. I don't think I would have left fishing, though, if you hadn't put the idea into my head. I couldn't see you go off on your own," said Stephen.

"Proper men are not sailors or fishermen," said Cyryl.

"What does that mean; proper men?" asked Stephen.

"Respectable men," said Cyryl.

"Being on land makes us respectable?" asked Stephen.

"More so, I think. Being a fisherman or a sailor is a common way of life. People look down on fishermen and sailors as poorer and ignorant fellows," said Cyryl. "Life at sea separates you from regular people."

"I hope when we leave here, we find a factory job somewhere or a way to make good money of our own as farmers. These Shakers make a nice profit from all their put up and selling," said Stephen. "I wouldn't want to return though, for another season."

"We'll move on in the spring or summer and find a better situation for us both," said Cyryl. "Ned said they could use us for spring planting and even summer work."

That evening both men wrote letters to their living parents, telling them of their new lives on land. These would be given to the farm deacon to be put with the other Shaker letters to be mailed. Cyryl told his father about the Shakers and his hopes of owning a farm. He told him about the scenic Upstate New York land of Appalachia and of his learning to read and write properly. An example of this was the very letter he was sending to his father. Cyryl thought of his Greek relatives including his sister and asked his father to send his love. The sentences in his letter were nominal in their wording, but expressed enough to show his new learning and what he wished to say to his father. Stephen Blome was more private in his letter writing and did not reveal its' contents. He was good at reading and writing and quickly wrote what seemed a short but serious message home. This letter addressed to his widowed mother.

Shaker Sister Rebecca's view of the outside world had been limited to trips to town to sell Shaker products. The town had fascinated and frightened her as well. Humanity certainly seemed different outside the Shaker Village. Some citizens were well-dressed and polite and others seemed crude and uneducated and even vulgar. People in town would stare at the Shakers as if from a foreign land. It made her feel odd and yet a certain personal pride would overtake her. She held her head high, not in a smug way but in a reverent way. She was a Shaker sister and conducted herself as such, a reflection of God's love. It was this that

111

Cyryl wanted to take away from her. What did she know of him? Nothing more than what he had told them upon arriving. Flattering words and charming ways could conceal a dark character. This life at sea was something she did not understand. He was a foreigner, and a Greek. They were known for violent tempers and roughness of all sorts. Fisherman and sailors had bad habits and often led lives of sin. She had heard a Shaker brother say so. But it was hard for her to imagine Cyryl as truly evil or bad. Although she did not know him, it just didn't seem to be a part of his character. In fact, she had wondered how he had survived his lonely life as a fisherman. Shaker Brother Isaac had stated that he showed a love of learning. He seemed so appreciative of the smallest gesture of kindness. No, he did not have a heart of evil or meanness. She remembered a Shaker sister's words that evil is easily exposed and the encouragement of goodness recognized as our lord God's reason for putting us here.

The sunrise that morning was gold. It shimmered along the horizon at first. And then filled the lower sky with sunlight, until the sun had risen above the tops of the pine trees. Now seen were the tree-covered hills fully formed.

That late April day, the sky turned dark and several inches of rain fell. The roads turned to mud and the grassy yards became soggy and soft under one's feet.

"We certainly have a wet day, today, said a Shaker sister. She was standing at a window in the parlor of a family house. The streams will swell. The brothers should be pleased. The sound of the falling rain against the roof and windows kept the sisters company as they went about their sewing.

"When I was a little girl, we lived in rural Massachusetts. I remember a rain storm so fierce, the lightening and wind brought down most of the trees in our farmyard. We had plenty of kindling that winter. And there was an elm tree I loved so, and its' branches were broken from the storm. How could God let such a thing happen I thought to myself, seeing the tree's branches splintered like that? I am in still in awe of what each season brings. I remember spring only once it arrives and mourn summer when fall commences. And winter is a wonder," said a Shaker sister.

"Sister, you should make a needlework depicting the seasons," said another Shaker sister.

"That is an idea! Yes, I will do that. It will be my special project. The four seasons."

An April rain made the flowers appear sooner than May. The land soggy and the leaves of foliage heavy with it. It brought a soothing sound, as if childhood was held within its' quiet torrent.

The month of April was the month of Cyryl' birthday. He had spent many of these alone but had always found a way to have a piece of cake. It was his way of celebrating. A few days before his birthday, and after some hesitation, he asked a Shaker brother if a cake could be made for him.

"I will speak to the Shaker sisters about it. I don't see why not. What kind of a cake?" asked the Shaker brother.

"Oh, any cake will do, chocolate or vanilla with frosting," said Cyryl, thinking of the prospect of a delicious Shaker cake.

"Let me speak to the sisters, Cyryl," said the Shaker brother.

The day of his birthday was requested and it was on this day that he was called into the large Shaker kitchen and there was his cake on a table, chocolate with vanilla frosting. The Shaker sisters sang happy birthday to him and he felt terribly embarrassed and grateful to the point of being emotional.

"Remember your birthday as a remembrance of Jesus and his miracle of walking on the sea. He had led you to us on land and we thank him for you are a blessing to us. You do good work the brothers tell us. Let the lord always be your guide whether on the sea or on land," said a Shaker sister.

Cyryl had not expected such eloquent spiritual words of advice at this moment. He could never be devout in that way. He suddenly felt the confines of their Shaker sect faith and the way it was represented in all things perfectly made or completed. To be one of them, a Shaker, meant to give your life and soul to their version of the lord. It was a strict and narrow view of life and as narrow and neat as the halls and stairs of their buildings; as symmetrical as the rows of windows and doors that represented an entrance to God's work. It was pressed with an iron, sanded to a fine finish, danced with almost irreverent emotion. The birthday cake was made with this same steady love and devotion. It was his gift. The birthday cake was cut into slices and after his insistence and everyone had a piece. It was moist and sugary sweet. He found the whole thing funny but only smiled at the thought. Then he saw Shaker Sister Rebecca standing at the edge of the room. Her face always seemed to hold a pleasant expression. He wondered about the reason as to why she were there. He knew they took in orphans. She was a poor orphan girl abandoned by heartless parents and left with the Shakers. She was an angel. He loved her at that moment. He must rescue her, he said to himself. He knew he wanted to see her again. She had looked at him several times as if sizing up his character. He could tell she was not around men often. Did he attract her as a man? He thought so, and he made a point of speaking in front of her, as close to her as possible. His voice had the unmistakable accent of a Greek. He gave her a dark intense look. She looked at him with surprise and then lowered her gaze to the floor. Her face no longer held a pleasant look but one that seemed troubled and almost sad. Then she looked up at him and appeared to hold herself higher than before. She now almost looked down at Cyryl. But her gaze at him changed from aloofness to a look of affection and bewilderment. He had won her over!

They had a chance meeting on the Shaker grounds and the following brief conversation was made.

"When did you become a Shaker Sister Rebecca?" asked Cyryl.

She seemed surprised by the question.

"It is not something I discuss with others but I will tell you Cyryl. I was adopted by the Shakers when I was just a small girl. My mother had died giving me birth and then my father passed away when I was nine years of age. He had been a preacher and he joined the Shakers after my mother's death. Then he died and I was left in the care of the Shaker brothers and sisters here."

"I am sorry to hear that you lost your mother and father at such a young age," said Cyryl.

"I never knew my mother but I am grateful that I have memories of my father. The Shakers say I was brought here as a gift from God. They have been very kind to me. It is the only home I know, although, I do wonder about the outside world from time to time. I am not sure my

114

mother would have wanted to be a Shaker. I have photographs of her. She looks too free-spirited and gay to be a Shaker." Shaker Sister Rebecca smiled.

"I am only guessing of course. I have a few of her letters that she wrote to father before they were married. She was very much in love with my father. Her parents owned a farm near New Lebanon. My father's family lived in town. His father, my grandfather had been a preacher as well," said Shaker Sister Rebecca.

"Do you have any living family?" asked Cyryl.

"I do but they are distant relatives and they now live farther out in the Midwest and Colorado. The Shakers are the only family I know." said Shaker Sister Rebecca.

Cyryl remained silent at first when he heard this but something inside of him told him to have the courage to speak at that moment.

Shaker Sister Rebecca then realized that she had told this workman too much about herself. She now regretted the telling of her personal story. She wanted to walk away but she stood motionless.

"Have you ever wanted to have your own family, Sister Rebecca?" asked Cyryl.

Shaker Sister Rebecca's face reddened at the question.

"My family is here, Cyryl. I am a Shaker woman, "said Shaker Sister Rebecca.

Cyryl went on with his words.

"But your mother was not a Shaker and you said yourself she might not have wanted to be one. You were not one as a small girl until your father brought you here. Do you want to stay?" asked Cyryl.

"Cyryl, this is not an appropriate subject for us to discuss. The weather or a pleasant exchange of words are fine but these questions make me feel awkward. We are a modest and very private people, Cyryl. You seem a good man and with a good heart. You need not be concerned for me," said Shaker Sister Rebecca.

"I am sorry if I offended you, Sister Rebecca. I felt I should ask you that question. I still feel you might consider it yourself someday," said Cyryl.

Shaker Sister Rebecca was now visibly upset.

115

"Cyryl, I think our conversation should end now." said Shaker Sister Rebecca abruptly.

She then walked off and Cyryl went his way as well.

The sunset of that day soon faded to dusk. The night sky filled with stars visible from the windows of the family houses. The night sounds of crickets, toads and an owl in one old oak tree had returned. Two Shaker sisters in one family house sat on chairs in the kitchen and talked before proceeding upstairs to bed. It had been a good day of work and prayer. It was Shaker Sister Clara and Shaker Sister Rebecca.

Shaker Sister Clara had dark blond hair that was always hidden by her Shaker cap and she was proud of its' thickness and naturally beautiful color. No one knew this except a few other Shaker sisters with whom she had shared this fact in more personal conversations of friendship and love. She had a good heart, but like the cap that kept her lovely hair hidden, her exterior manner, although always Christian in spirit and gesture, could be stern and swift. She was the best worker you could imagine, but if the task overwhelmed her, she had to be reminded to not fuss too much over the result. She knew this about herself but it was as if she were looking from a distance at her own person, a good Shaker and a Christian, who grew agitated or excited too quickly. But what completed her character in the most ironic way, was the steady and articulate process at which she approached all tasks. No one could sew or mend, or bake or assemble a project like Shaker Sister Clara. When she sang her voice, though small and restrained, was pleasant and sweet, and it never missed the correct tune of a note. It was a most accurate reflection of her soul. Past middle age, she wore glasses now, and she always kept them with her, slowly placing them on her face after a careful wiping of the glass in each prescribed lens. She was intelligent and thoughtful and she always seemed to give the best advice. When she spoke of her mother and father or her siblings while recalling the family and growing up with them in rural New York, tears would often fill her eyes, even when the story seemed to not have a melancholy element or a loss in it. It was the act of remembering that had brought such emotion to her. You had to wonder if she were truly happy as a Shaker, but she often expressed her strong belief and faith and loyalty to the Shaker faith and message. Beneath her steady but easily excitable façade was a great

116

passion. She would have made a wonderful wife and mother, and a great actress according to Shaker Sister Emily, who meant this in a most complimentary way.

The sky was still visible between white clouds in the sky. An opening of it clear and blue. Shaker Sister Rebecca had cut flowers in the Shaker garden; tulips and roses. The afternoon light fading and the land losing the light of day. She lifted her Shaker skirt to avoid sullying it on the wet earth. How delicate the blooms looked in their colors of red and pale pink. She would try to capture their image in a needlepoint. But she knew it was not possible. Not in the way she saw them at that moment in the light of the garden.

"Sister Rebecca, have you finished the needle point you had started? The needle point piece showing the calendar months of the year and flowers from our Shaker garden?" asked Shaker Sister Clara.

"Oh, no, Sister Clara, I have a lot more work to do on that one. It now has dark green leaves as well, which I placed around some of the flowers," said Shaker Sister Rebecca.

"You will have to show it to me in the morning. You do the best needlework I have ever seen! My favorite is still the one with bluebells and the scripture from Psalms," said Shaker Sister Clara.

"That is the one I gave to you as a present," said Shaker Sister Rebecca.

"Yes, my very favorite. Goodnight, my dearest," said Shaker Sister Clara.

"Goodnight, Sister Clara."

Shaker Sister Rebecca had wanted to mention her encounter with Cyryl the Greek hired workman to Shaker Sister Clara. But she was fearful that Cyryl might get into some trouble with the Shaker brothers for his brash actions and questions. The Shaker sisters rarely spoke to the workmen. Her brief conversation with this man had left her with questions about her own life at the Shaker community. It had made her ask the question of whether she wished to have a family and a life outside of the Shaker community, now that she was a young woman and faced with the possibility of it. It would be in her thoughts and prayers.

That week, work and prayer proceeded as it always had. An early evening meeting had brought Shaker brothers and sisters together. As a Shaker brother prayed, a rain storm outside grew stronger. It now seemed to compete with the words of the prayer being spoken. Hail began to fall and beat against the roof of the building. The sound of it was turbulent and incessant. It tore leaves from the trees and filled the air with them. Small branches from the trees brittle enough to break off from the force of wind, hail and rain also fell victim to the torrent and now covered the ground. They continued to pray fervently and after a few minutes the beating sound of hail subsided and all grew quiet outside. It was as if an illness had been healed or a weak spirit strengthened. The prayer ended in a peaceful amen. One area of sky cleared and showed sunlight low in the sky. No rainbow was seen; only the beginning of dusk and the remaining leaves on the trees almost colorless in the fading light.

As the weather grew warmer, the fields between the orchards of trees changed from gray and brown to green and gold. The earth underfoot was still soggy from a rain. The raindrops on sedge grass and weeds shimmered in the morning sunlight.

One morning before Cyryl was to go out to the fields to work, Harren the farm deacon called him into his office. He was very polite but serious in his speech to Cyryl.

"I have been told by a Shaker member that you have approached Shaker Sister Rebecca on more than one occasion," said Harren.

Cyryl thought for a moment and then replied.

"Yes, there was a day I went into town to get a few things and I knocked on the kitchen door to see if she might need something," said Cyryl.

"You were dressed as if you were attempting to court her. It is not allowed to socialize with the Shaker sisters unless invited to do so," said Harren. His voice now seemed impatient and forceful.

"I only wanted to express my appreciation for their kindness to me," said Cyryl. He was now flush with anger but tried to hide the fact. The problem was that Cyryl's emotions clearly showed on his face.

"Shaker Sister Rebecca is young and attractive and that makes your actions even more of a concern. Please mind what you say to the Shaker brothers and sisters. Know your place. If you want to socialize you should do it in town. What about your friend Stephen? Bring him along to keep you company," said Harren.

"Yes, I could do that," said Cyryl. "Or I could ask Bill or Ned."

"That's your decision," said Harren. And with that Cyryl went off to work as usual. Stephen had noticed that Cyryl had been called into the farm deacon's office and catching up with him, he asked Cyryl what had been discussed. He explained it all to Stephen but he seemed displeased with Cyryl.

"I don't understand you! We will lose our place here. I thought we had decided to stay until the end of summer. We don't have enough saved to head out yet," said Stephen.

"I was only being polite and trying to act as a gentleman," said Cyryl. There was more to it than what he had told Stephen, but it was hard to explain his feelings as he wasn't sure of them himself. He was in defiance of something and he wasn't sure what it was. Perhaps, he was trying to prove himself a man. Shaker Sister Rebecca was a woman he should not approach. She was the forbidden fruit. In truth, his actions with Shaker Sister Rebecca were a sort of acting out, of something that he had to experience; something that he learned as a child, that was a part of tradition and the expression of love.

IX

Spring

Spring came on a day. There were green sprouts of growth in the earth. New leaves on the trees now visible against an overcast sky that would dissipate to blue. A few flowers were in bloom in the gardens. There was the sight and sound of bees and birds and a gentle wind bringing nature to sway.

The warm, early afternoon sunlight shined down onto the Shaker family houses. The green grass in the yard was no longer wet with morning dew. The eggs had been gathered from the chicken coop. The kitchen floor had been mopped. It smelled of sudsy lye soap. Cream was ladled from the top of the milk cans. Chickens, crickets and bees made their noises of clucking and chirping and buzzing against the quiet sound of day. The sky had settled for a mix of white clouds and a pale-blue sky.

That next morning the rising sun shined behind the black branches of trees along a hilltop; the light of it thrown onto the valley fields below made green colors mustard and orange.

Spring was always a miracle of new growth seen in lime-green outgrowths and yellow or purple wildflowers amongst grass and milkweed rods. Between the trees a creek had thawed. It flowed smoothly over moss-covered rocks and pebbles the color of sand and copper. The sunlight reflected off its liquid surface as if moving light reflection; flashes and glints of white, red and prisms. A shadow cast over it would reveal its shallow bed and the movement of frogs, small fish or turtles.

"There is much work to be done. Let's open the windows to let the fresh air indoors. It rained yesterday and we will have extra work to do in the garden. Did you see the purple irises in bloom? That's something to see!" said a Shaker sister.

"The roses are in bloom; pinks and red," said another Shaker sister.

The silhouette of tree trunks and leaf-covered branches framed the blue sky. A yellow in the fields showed the growth of new weeds and wild flowers after a recent rain fall and several days of sunshine. Spring was rebirth and renewal; a rebirth of spiritual faith as well.

That evening Cyryl had a dream. What he remembered of it was made of sunlight reflecting off the surface of the sea and the sight of sea birds. He thought it a good omen as sunlight made things grow and birds represented land. The new growth of the spring planting had made neat green rows in the plowed Shaker fields. Small green apples and pears appeared between young leaves on the fruit trees. Blackberries still green would soon grow large, deep purple and ripe and worth the chance of prickling by thorns on their branches. Grass never looked greener or dandelions more sour yellow. Spring was a miracle of blooms; the unseen movement of growth during rain and sunshine and rise and fall of cool nights.

In the early morning hours of the day, a thunderstorm had broken over the Appalachian hills. The roads were muddy and the fields were heavy with rainfall. The sun appeared from behind gray clouds creating a strange shadow onto one of the white wood family houses. The grass in the yard had grown much taller and new blooms on flowers had appeared yellow and red. The washing, sewing, cleaning and cooking were done by the Shaker sisters. Herbs were picked in the garden. Now the sun had begun to fade. The Shaker brothers had returned from their work. It was time for a Shaker dinner.

Cyryl had now worked on land since the previous fall. He felt different as a man. His life had changed much and for the better he felt. The sky above the land was large and open with bright white and yellow sunrises and mystical pink sunsets. The valleys were a patchwork of greens, lime and emerald, tinged with yellow or blue. In the spring after the snow had melted away in the warm sunlight, the brown leaves of fall were again visible on the ground under the trees. They were an assortment of small and large, giant-like, young or ancient, with stencil leaf patterns of curves, sloping points and interior veins that connected to stems. The spring wind blew them in light lifting swirls, tossing them aside as fresh green buds appeared on the trees and among the grass and twigs on the ground. All that was dormant had returned as if these plants and flowers had hidden themselves against the great cold wind and snow of winter.

The once frozen ground yielded to the plow and shovel. Rain brought mud and blurred views from windows of the land in transformation. The land was life itself. Not just the land but the sky as well, seen above its contours of valley and hill.

Cyryl knew why the Shakers had chosen this place. It was surely a place where God existed no matter the season. It was a mystical place too, a place where folk-lore would arise in oral tales from past generations. You imagined the men and women of past centuries working the land and living day to day until their Christian or damned souls returned to the sky. Something about this place always gave you the hope of salvation, even if salvation was just a spring day like the one before you. The present season, year and the era seemed to remember the past and seemed conscious of the future. Seasons looked much the same as before although the species of things had grown perhaps less lush in their range of color and bloom. The future would bring cleared land and fewer trees, more human construction and a loss of light and shadow that had once patterned this untouched Appalachian area. The sun would again warm the land and the sky would reflect the land and the events of the season, however simple.

There was a history to this rural place, unlike the history of a town or city. There were no famous individuals to reference, only ordinary men and women who were not so ordinary if we were to have known them better. These were Americans who had lived and died here. Some had given their lives for the new-found freedom of the American colonies separate from British rule. The sons of some had given their lives fighting during the recent Civil War. But most had lived here peacefully and had prospered enough to have sustained themselves throughout many a season. Their spirit remained along with that of the Indian. Their mark left in the land, in the shape of the trees or the sound made when a wind blew over it.

The wind stirred the grass in the field like a surge in the sea. The rolling hills were a pale green that day. The sky was a wash of blue and with white shapeless clouds. Cyryl could sense something magical in this Appalachian place. The shades cast against the land would shift and move with the daylight. A sudden breeze brought green and brown leaves into the air but at only a small distance. It was alive with something spiritual and lasting, almost a prophecy of earth and sky. It was a good place and he would miss it, for he knew at some point he would continue to another. He hoped it was not too far in time and distance, for he longed for something of his own. He said a silent prayer in direction of this hope and headed back to the Shaker community.

Now as if overnight, all trees had budded green. The sun warmed the earth. The work of spring planting began. There was much to do and Cyryl and Stephen felt no reason to leave. Here was the opportunity to learn about planting and farming of the land. They were caught up in it. The beauty of the place in the bloom of spring surprised them. The crops grew, as crops grow in the spring, as if without us noticing. Where fields of plain plowed earth were just a short memory before, there now grew fine long rows of green leafy fruit and vegetables. The rows of vertical green gave one an example of what men and women on this earth could sew and cultivate; the steady work of human hands that covered the fields in a quilt of precise labor. A distance from the planted fields, the hilly landscape was thick with birch and pine trees. To the West, the sky glowed with a hazy sunlight.

There was another chance meeting with Shaker Sister Rebecca on a day when Cyryl had been asked to help with labors near a family house. Shaker Sister Rebecca, seeing Cyryl stopped for a moment and looked at him and then looked out towards the planted fields. They were a short distance from each other but Cyryl came no closer to her. In her hands, she held a Shaker basket. It was a beautiful spring day. She waved to him; looked out towards his figure, shielding her eyes from the sun. The ritual of courtship seemed between them, to be acted upon and yet, they seemed confined to their very specific roles, both spiritual and economic. The made a beautiful couple, and if you had seen them close to one another, you would have acknowledged it as so. Both were young, physically attractive and of a sweet nature. She then turned and went on her way towards the family house where she dwelled and Cyryl headed out to his work.

A short time of a few days had passed. Shaker Sister Rebecca sat on her bed. She had removed her bonnet and kerchief from her neck. She was on the verge of tears. A Shaker sister entered the room and asked Shaker Sister Rebecca what was the matter?

"What is it dear Sister Rebecca? You look so very sad."

"My heart is broken Sister Clara. To have doubt…I feel I am no longer worthy of being a Shaker," said Shaker Sister Rebecca.

"You are not worthy? What has happened that you would doubt yourself as a Shaker sister?" asked Shaker Sister Clara.

Shaker Sister Rebecca now had tears in her eyes.

"Cyryl, our Greek hired workman who was a fisherman. He has made me question my Shaker faith," said Shaker Sister Rebecca.

"I have even imagined us together as man and wife," said Shaker Sister Rebecca. "He is of a kind nature and attractive in features. Did I tell you of the day, he came to the door of our kitchen all dressed in his best clothes to ask if I might need something before he went into town? He did this. I thought someone must have noticed," said Shaker Sister Rebecca. She was smiling at the memory of it. But then her face grew solemn again as she questioned her future as a Shaker sister.

"What shall I do?" asked Shaker Sister Rebecca. She appeared at that moment, once again, a little orphaned girl to Shaker Sister Clara.

"Oh, Sister Rebecca you surprise me…You are still very young. I am older than you," said Shaker Sister Clara. "A Shaker member lives his or her life each day at a time, Sister Rebecca. We are not certain of even the next day or of God's continued grace. So, for you to assume a whole life as a Shaker, is assuming too much! A Shaker life is a hard one and a lonely one too. It does not surprise me that you, a young and pretty woman, might have doubts about staying at Mount Lebanon. You can love God in all places and a family life and children are such a blessing, just as you were a blessing to us, when you arrived at so young an age. How lively you were and how much we loved to see your shining face each day. You must decide for yourself Sister Rebecca. There are no guarantees in life. Now is a time for prayer and reflection. I do know, that if you wish to someday leave here, we will do what we can to give you a good start. It is what your reverend father wished for you. He said you might wish to leave here someday," said Shaker Sister Clara.

"He spoke of this?" asked Shaker Sister Rebecca.

"Yes, he said your mother could never have been a Shaker sister. It is one of the reasons he did not join us, until after her death," said Shaker Sister Clara.

"He did not tell me this," said Shaker Sister Rebecca.

"He wanted you to find your own way. Now pray to the Lord and ask for guidance dear Rebecca. I will say nothing to no one until you decide. I too will pray," said Shaker Sister Clara

"Sister, say nothing of Cyryl to the others. He will surely lose his work here," said Shaker Sister Rebecca.

"I will say nothing to the other Shaker brothers or sisters," said Shaker Sister Clara."

A fog had settled over the land. It covered in mist, the view of the planted rows of corn and beans, wheat, squash and potatoes. The vegetable and herb garden near the main buildings had also disappeared into a dense white cloud of moisture, as if God wished to veil the land in solitude, limiting our human sight to the immediate and ourselves. But as morning progressed, it burned off and the warm sun once again illuminated the same place that was familiar; where hands dug into the earth clearing it of weeds. It was the kind of work that was most satisfying because you were close to the earth, the smell of it, and you a part of it in the simplest way possible. You would return to it someday and perhaps be reborn. The bible reminded us of this.

The land was wet with an early morning rain. The dirt roads muddy and hard to travel. But still the daily work of the village had to be completed and there was much work to do.

The workmen and the Shaker brothers and sisters shared one thing equally and that was the natural setting of Mount Lebanon, New York. The beauty of the place changed with the weather and the season. It could be wet and soggy one day and sunny and dry another. The green of trees in a cloud of rain could look almost blue. The blue sky turned to gray without noticing until the shadows they brought changed the tone and color of the landscape as well. It was God's way of bringing equality to their lives. The sound of rain or wind and the feeling one gets when seeing the trees covering a hill turn to fall colors of red, gold, brown and

125

yellow. These were the images that framed the manmade buildings and the planted fields.

The activity of the day was at full energy. The workmen had been assigned different tasks by each of the Shaker families and were now heading to or were at their fields, barns or adjoining buildings associated with Shaker industry, handmade crafts and the care of animals. This was a rural life Cyryl had not seen before. It was truly American in all its aspects. The buildings and the style in which all was done here impressed him. It was simple and honest and represented a truth about life and the meaning of it, although Cyryl would not have been able to put it into these words exactly. That meaning would have been seeing the results of good work and self-discipline.

Cyryl worked in the field that day with the Shaker brothers. The rows of crops needed weeding and watering. There would be more planting that week, cucumber and squash seeds. There was always a chore or a project of some sort that he needed to assist with. The village was short of men. It was one of the reasons they had taken him in. It was a growing problem in the Shaker community but he had never heard them complain about it. It was a problem that must have worried them. The outside world was changing fast. The Shakers had seen their numbers shrink in other Shaker villages. All communities were short of men and sometimes women did tasks that had always been assigned to the Shaker brothers.

Cyryl walked a trail about a quarter mile from where he had worked that day, just to see the area at the edge of the fields. Bugs and butterflies flew and fluttered in the air above the field. At the edge of the woods and under the trees grew grass, weeds and a wildflower with gold and brown centered buds that looked like miniature sunflowers. Cyryl looked into the woods. Sunlight cast down through the tall branches of the trees created an eerie pattern of illumination on the floating flora covering the floor of the woods. It was not unlike the sunlight he had seen cast from the windows of a Catholic church onto the rows of seating. He stood unmoving and then decided to return to the narrow trail he had followed to this place. Then he saw a man walking further down the trail he had followed. Not a Shaker brother or one of the laborers from the community, but a local farmer from the area. He wore overalls and a baggy shirt that must have been white once but was now a faded gray. He wore a hat with a brim and he carried a hoe. The farmer was now a distance from Cyryl and then soon, he was gone over a hill to another field. The sun was still brilliant in the sky even though it was late afternoon. He headed back down the trail to his dinner and some rest. There was always a good meal waiting for him with plenty of bread. Bill would have a story to tell, maybe about the day or about Pennsylvania. Cyryl had told his stories before, about his Greek family and his growing up in New York City. They even knew his favorite food; feta cheese and olives on Greek bread.

In one of the family houses, a Shaker sister sitting on a ladder back chair put on her spectacles and began to sew pieces of fabric together to be used for a quilt. Sunlight streamed through the windows of the room casting its' light onto the walls and sparse furnishings. The brilliant light partially covered her figure in a slant of illumination that she used to work her needle into the fabric, creating a neat line of stitched thread that connected the simple patterned fabrics. It was a pleasant task to her and she enjoyed stopping to admire the work she had completed, half folded on her lap.

It was early evening and Cyryl was returning from the fields after a day's work. He heard his name being called and he looked back down the slight hill he had just ascended. The same hill he always climbed on his way back to the hired men's residence building.

"Cyryl! Wait up a minute!"

It was workman Ned calling out to him and as Cyryl looked back he saw Ned quicken his pace as he made his way up the hill to where Cyryl was standing. It was the first time that Cyryl noticed how Ned seemed almost twisted in his physical being. It was something he hid from others, but Cyryl could now see it in his lopsided physical effort in climbing the hill. With the setting sun behind Ned's approaching figure, it was something Cyryl would remember his whole life; the malformed physicality of a man exerting his person through the daily act of living.

"I think I got myself a place in town," said Ned, with an excited look on his slender, handsome face.

"What do you mean Ned?" asked Cyryl.

127

"Well, I've got a job in a store in New Lebanon town lined up for myself. It sells general goods; dry goods and such. I am going to help run the place and live in my own rooms above the store," said Ned.

"Ned, that sounds great. How did you land such a position for yourself?" asked Cyryl.

"Well, I'm not supposed to tell you that," said Ned. He wore a slight frown as he contemplated this thought. "If I do, it might spoil it for me. But all the same, I think it is pretty set and all," said Ned.

"Ned, you'll be a man about town. You'll wear nice silk vests and smoke expensive cigars!" said Cyryl, with a smile.

"I can't smoke. I never could; weak lungs. But a nice silk vest would be nice. Look, don't say anything to Bill or the others. I don't want any jealousy or talk," said Ned.

"I won't say a word about it. That's great Ned. It will be our secret," said Cyryl.

The Shaker sisters were at work in their kitchen and thinking of the meals they would need to serve that day and week.

"I am looking forward to some of your tomato jam, sister," said Shaker Sister Emily.

"I will bring in some more water from the well. We will need a few more gallons for cooking," said a Shaker sister.

"I think the kitchen is the coolest place in the house. That is when the stove isn't cooking. It doesn't get a direct sunlight," said another Shaker sister.

More trips were made to nearby Mount Lebanon and other New York State towns to sell Shaker goods and make purchases for the Shaker village. Cyryl went on several of these buying and selling trips and it gave him a chance to see the countryside of New York and its rural and smaller urban environments. He was impressed by the neatness of the small towns. They all looked very well-planned and you could see a certain pride was taken in the courthouses and lawns and trees that lined the streets and avenues. The architecture was a mix of Victorian and Colonial, American Classic Revival, Georgian, Gothic and Beaux Arts styles. But Cyryl could not guess the specific style of the turrets, bay windows, curves and decorative facades and aspects of these buildings.

But he greatly admired their imaginative and unique use of building materials and the integrity of the buildings in their solid makings.

X

Early Summer

Summer brought a heat and the maturity of crops that had advanced with the sun and rain. There was the soil as a reminder of what rooted all things. At day's end, a retreating when the sunlight left the sky.

It was the bright month of June. The days had grown warmer and wild flowers in the untilled valley fields bejeweled the familiar green of sedge grass and weeds. When it had rained, the clouds had looked a blue-gray and the clear blue sky of early summer had disappeared behind this melancholy cover. The crop fields had been planted and rows of Shaker seeds growing new and yet without bloom, lined the freshly-tilled earth.

The summer would warm and grow hotter as it entered the July month. There would be mild days and other days of humidity and weather too hot for comfort and lacking a cool breeze. But towards evening, the cooler temperatures came and you forgot the day's heat and punishing sun. This was the best part of summer and the most memorable as the dark of night, an evening meal and the pleasure of conversation uninterrupted by work or unrelated to it, was, along with wages earned, your reward for a day's labor.

It was now past mid-July. Shaker sisters bowed towards the earth to pick peppers that grew in neat green rows. They wore modest, comfortable clothing much the same in design but made of different fabrics. Long-sleeved attire fashioned from a finely-woven cotton in a solid color or sometimes with a printed pattern. A light fabric cap was worn that tied under the chin and so covered the face as to make it difficult to determine young or old; the age of the wearer. For what was the use of human conceit regarding the lord's purpose for their lives? Time was to be made use of and aging was an earthly conclusion.

Above them small white clouds were scattered in a Dutch blue sky. The summer heat brought out bugs and butterflies. Weeds bloomed

130

rouge and yellow colors. Birds in small flocks found resting places on the branches of trees. A Shaker garden was a sight to see. In full maturity, it had a remarkable leafy appearance between its' clean rows of dark rich soil.

Green pine trees and the lighter green color of maple, beech and elm leaves formed a barrier along the verge of a field. The sky was a wisp of white clouds mixed with a blue sky.

Later that day, Cyryl and Stephen shared a view of rain clouds that had formed above the distant hills. Soon the rain would stop their work. It came in torrents leaving the men to run for cover in a Shaker building nearby. It soaked the freshly tilled earth and corn crops. A bright glowing light of sunset shined pink and yellow above the surrounding hills of Mount Lebanon. Soon the sun had set almost completely and then night fell over the wet rain-soaked land. One minute the landscape familiar and then dark and unrecognizable. It must have been like this long ago when the American Indians inhabited these hills and valleys. The sun would return in the morning and look and bright as it had that past morning, that is if the lord willed it.

The following morning was damp and chilly. Behind the branches of the trees the sky was pink as dusk. Cyryl and the Shaker brothers went to the field early that morning to weed between the rows of corn and wheat. The soil was turned and the crops watered.

That day Cyryl worked again in the fields. The crops had been planted and were thriving under a bright sunshine. It was his job to pull the weeds that had sprouted up around the plant. It was a common job. The job of any farmer tending to his land; the thought pleased him. He had become a farmer in America. His hands now tended his crops. He had become a part of the land and the sea now seemed a far-away memory of glittering green-blue liquid. The lonely docks and nights that made the brick buildings look gray. He thought of his fisherman friends. How impressed they would be! Cyryl now a real farmer and no longer the sailor-fisherman; they would have a good laugh about it.

It was now a Sunday and a day of rest for the Shaker village. Cyryl stayed indoors resting and thought about things. He made plans for his life. He imagined the farm he would own one day and the fine parcel of land that he would own. He imagined the wife he would marry and their children. He would warn his son about the sea. The life of a fisherman was hard and lonely. No better yet, he would never mention it at all.

In the distance, the green colors of the surrounding hills and Appalachian valley looked vibrant and glowing. The colors of the dahlia garden flowers that were orange and red and bright yellow, the green leaves of the basil and parsley, the white wash on the buildings, the red of brick; these all seemed brighter somehow. Black, white, gray and blue were colors seen in the clothing of the Shakers always in motion. Brown was found in tree branches and the varnish that stained a wood. The clouds above in a blue sky were as white as they could possibly be; dust and wood colors; the sound of a metal latch or a creaking weather vane changing direction because of the wind. The reflection of sunlight against a glass window-pane, the color of white and gold, were also a part of the rural place.

That early evening Cyryl walked back to his lodgings. Looking out at the setting sun beyond the fields, a vision of the sea came to him again, dark and vast and with a dull light gleaming on its surface. The land returned before him, now fading into night. Cyryl looked out at the last light of sunset beyond the hills. Its' color and aura was never quite the same on any given evening and yet, it always appeared at the end of a day as a natural occurrence. Each day on land offering something new.

It was a day like heaven for the sun shone brightly above in the sky, an almost cloudless sky of blue. John Michael was at work in the fields tending to the crops. Doing fine in the Appalachian sunshine and irrigation water brought down from the hills. He stopped to look up and then in a distance he saw them. He could not be mistaken. I was his brother Josiah with a woman and two children. He stood looking with great surprise and then he ran towards Josiah and they embraced. It was that day in heaven that one of the Shaker brothers had predicted. Josiah had returned alive and it was a miracle.

Josiah had escaped to the North but because of fear and the bitterness inside of him that he could not totally explain, he had remained separate from his family. He thought his mother and father to be ignorant people. An example of the abuse white people had brought to African

132

Americans. Most African Americans longed for freedom and his parents did too, they had said, but only God could bring such freedom. Ignorant he thought them and he still had a fierce bitterness in his heart. John Michael had acquired wisdom and he spoke to his brother Josiah with the hope of his understanding the past and looking to a better future.

"Josiah," he said. "The idea of individual liberty makes racial prejudice unimportant. That idea must win over hatred and ignorance. Some people just aren't smart enough to accept that fact or they're scared not knowing what the future might bring. It was like this with our parents; too scared or ignorant to change or to see the possibility of change," said John Michael.

That evening the only light in the sky was along the hill-shaped horizon. It cast no light directly onto the valley below that had faded to an olive-green shadow. Nightfall and its' sound of crickets followed quickly. Fireflies lit up the air. It was time to go indoors.

Cyryl traveled with the Shakers to sell goods and visit another Shaker village in Watervliet, New York. Shaker Sister Rebecca and several other Shaker sisters also went along on this trip to town. There were several stores that offered a variety of goods along the town's main street. One store offered pharmaceutical items, some displayed in its window. Glass in clear, pale green or blue, bubbled and shaped and pressed with identifying letters or numbers or with a paper label, held potions, remedies, shampoos, miracle cures and cleaners of all sorts. The vessel as important as the contents until emptied. It then became a false advertisement for whatever it promised. In this same window was displayed a postal card with a view of Niagara Fall.

Out of curiosity, Shaker Sister Rebecca looked in the window of a dress shop. There was a shapely female mannequin wearing a pretty, white ruffled blouse of the latest style with a flowing skirt below. Another mannequin wore a dress with a slim waist and a full skirt. It was made of a cream-color cotton and was draped with more cotton fabric with an embroidery stitching along its' edges. The same embroidered draping decorated the sleeves and created a lacy effect along the shoulders. She had never seen such a lovely dress. Shaker Sister Rebecca had never allowed herself to look at worldly clothes of the non-Shakers, but something inside of her challenged her to look at that instant. She

133

imagined herself wearing the pretty clothes and a feeling of guilty pleasure came over her. She looked a short distant from herself at a little boy with dark hair standing and looking with curiosity at her. She forgot that it was her Shaker clothes that made him look with such interest. Suddenly his mother appeared and took his hand. The mother starred at Shaker Sister Rebecca and told the little boy something. Then she urged the child on, on to their shopping and other errands. Shaker Sister Rebecca knew little about this secular existence. She only knew of the outside world from what she had been told by the Shaker sisters and brothers. A thought of her own mother came to her mind. Would she, a reverend's wife worn such a blouse and skirt? Perhaps she might have dressed this way as a young girl. She often made up fantasies of her mother and tried to imagine her as she would have been when living. Her mother had been as pretty as Shaker Sister Rebecca was now. But she only had one photograph of her mother and in it she is wearing a dark-colored dress, and more elegant than what was in the dressmaker's window. Shaker Sister Rebecca caught herself, realizing she had wasted time daydreaming and quickly went to find the Shaker sisters who were selecting fabrics for their sewing projects. Idle hands and day dreaming were not desirable traits for a Shaker woman, no matter the age.

Shaker Sister Clara was a light sleeper and woke to the sound of a creaking door opening. She looked out of her room and found Shaker Sister Rebecca standing in the hallway in her night clothes holding a candle."

"What is the matter child?" asked Shaker Sister Clara.

"I am getting a cup of water," said Shaker Sister Rebecca.

"What is troubling you?" asked Shaker Sister Clara.

"How do you know I am troubled?" asked Shaker Sister Rebecca.

"You seemed so today. Have you spoken to the lord about it? Something has put a cloud over your mind. You seemed impatient with Shaker Sister Emily in the kitchen. You never show that kind of ill feeling towards anyone and certainly not towards our dear Sister Emily."

"Oh, was I being unpleasant or rude? I did not think so at the time. Yes, I am unsettled but it is not something I think I can talk about," said Shaker Sister Rebecca.

"We can all talk freely here. You must mean it is too personal a subject," said Shaker Sister Clara.

"Yes, that is what I am trying to say. There are some things better left to ourselves and the lord our savior," said Shaker Sister Rebecca.

"Do you not want to be in this room?" asked Shaker Sister Clara.

"I felt thirsty for water, that is all" said Shaker Sister Rebecca.

"Is the room you are in not suitable for you? You might let in some fresh air. It is warm outside this evening," said Shaker Sister Clara.

"I felt the need to rise and move about a bit," said Shaker Sister Rebecca.

"A prayer to God would be a remedy," said Shaker Sister Clara.

"You return to bed. I will be fine. I will return to sleep and say a prayer," said Shaker Sister Rebecca.

"Good night then sister," said Shaker Sister Clara.

"Good night. Jesus loves you."

Shaker Sister Rebecca did finally sleep, but fitfully.

That next morning, Shaker Sister Rebecca looked out over the land. The sun was rising but because it was early morning things like trees and buildings and fences were still silhouettes of themselves. It was cold enough to remind you of the shelter of housing. What was the morning telling Shaker Sister Rebecca? That all things were possible within human will and a persevering spirit.

Near a Shaker building grew a thin rosebush. A few scarlet red roses were in bloom on its branches. No other flowers grew alongside this building and the flowering bush had always looked lonely and out of place. It wasn't a part of any garden spot. It had simply been planted sometime previous and had thrived. Shaker Sister Rebecca had always loved it for it always bloomed each summer and sometimes even after a snowfall. It was a silent, sturdy friend. It cheered her on gray days when her heart was heavy with self-doubt and weariness.

Cyryl realized that his dream of having a farm and a piece of land included the idea of an idyllic union of marriage and children. Just as his own Greek parents had met, fallen in love and had a family. It should be like this, he thought. It was something the Shakers had decided against in their own personal choice of living. For Cyryl, this idea of male and female union represented true happiness and tradition. But it was a distant thought, clouded by the realities of his sexual identity and desires. And yet, he felt a need to, at the very least, act out or upon this ideal image of marriage and children and observe the result. And so, he would take a great risk and let Sister Rebecca know that he found her attractive and that he was a man with a future to be determined. He would be Cicero at that moment, making a speech that held significance in its' expression of love.

All of what he thought to be sweet and innocent was in that moment. The blue sky and green land and Shaker Sister Rebecca standing there at a distance near the roses, young and pretty. He imagined them as man and wife. A family and farm came to mind. His vision of the perfect American union and setting. It was timeless and simple as it should be. Lovely in its' completion and traditional overture. He approached her and she looked over at him.

"Marry me, Rebecca and let me take you away with me. We will have a good life together," said Cyryl.

Cyryl stood a short distance to her and she responded to his words without looking at him.

"You do not know what it means to be a Shaker. It isn't something you just discard. I will not betray my faith. It would be best for you to go," said Shaker Sister Rebecca.

"And they will send me away. That is no solution to the feelings in my heart," said Cyryl.

"Yes, that would be best," said Shaker Sister Rebecca.

"Where is your faith Rebecca? It cannot exist outside of this place?" asked Cyryl.

"God is in all places, Cyryl," said Shaker Sister Rebecca,

"Then God is with us in this. I believe it," said Cyryl.

"You corrupt my thoughts Cyryl and I will not allow it."

"I love you," said Cyryl.

"There are higher purposes in life than one's own desires," said Shaker Sister Rebecca. She went on to explain her feelings and what she said, she had never told another person before that moment.

"I often wonder what it would have been like to have lived outside of the Shaker community; if my parents were living," said Shaker Sister Rebecca.

"I imagine the three of us living us in a regular kind of house; a two-story house with a porch and front yard, full of flowers like the ones you see in New Lebanon. I would have worn ribbons in my hair. I would have worn lace dresses on special occasions like weddings and at my birthday parties. I suppose it was normal to imagine and wonder about this as a child. But as I grew older, I began to scold myself when those thoughts came into my mind. I was a Shaker child, raised to believe that my life was dedicated to Christ the Lord and a member of this community of Shaker believers. It wasn't until I met you, Cyryl, that I began to question my identity as a Shaker sister. I was angry at you at first, but now I realize that it was not your fault but the result of circumstance. I had not met a man like you before, a non-Shaker man, charming and attractive and that was the beginning of my spiritual doubt. I know that you would make a good husband for me, but I cannot accept your proposal of marriage. I think God wishes me to follow my heart and my spiritual duty. You have shown yourself to be of a kind nature and with a loving heart," said Shaker Sister Rebecca.

Cyryl was overcome with emotion after hearing this and so he said nothing for a few moments but simply looked at Rebecca with sad eyes.

"So, you wish to remain here?" he asked.

"Yes, but if I were to marry a man, it would certainly be someone like you Cyryl," said Shaker Sister Rebecca.

"I will leave here. I will find my own way as I must," said Cyryl.

He left her and returned to the workmen's residence.

The opening of the box had become another ritual, not unlike the many Shaker Sister Rebecca performed as a Shaker sister. But this time, an overwhelming feeling of despair overtook her. She had never really known her mother. Her father had been dead since she was a small child. She felt cheated and angry and despite knowing better in her heart she felt hurt by them for abandoning her. They had not loved her enough. They didn't care for her. This she knew was not true; in her heart, she knew it to be false. But she allowed herself to feel and think it anyway. It was a way of putting the box from the past away forever. Material objects were of no real value. Bits of ribbon, jewelry, precious photographs were nothing compared to the love and memories we held in our hearts and mind. She knew she must forgive them.

It was a day of sunshine and yet, it seemed hidden somewhere beyond the green hills that framed the valley land of this Shaker place. Shaker Sister Rebecca walked across the field with no destination in mind. Now she was certain of her feelings. She loved this place. It had always been her home. The sky above the field was a mix of blue sky and gray clouds. The trees on the hills looked dark and green.

She knew that this time would come, when she would have to decide whether to stay at the Shaker village or make her own way outside of the community. It was the only place she had known. But somehow, she knew in her heart she might someday leave. It had always been a part of her thinking and she had not fully realized it, until that very moment. Now it seemed obvious to her. It strengthened her faith. The memories of her childhood came to her, the taste of sweet molasses and the many flowers that bloomed with the vegetables in the Shaker garden, these superior to the wild flowers in the fields. A feeling of pain and anguish came over Shaker Sister Rebecca without warning. It was such a great pain that she thought she might not endure it and tears came to her eyes. The only thing that she could compare it to might be the feeling a Christian might feel at the thought of the lord's crucifixion. But it was her own emotional pain that she was feeling and she knew what its' origin was right away. It was the sorrow and loss she had stored away since a young girl, of her being an orphan. During her whole childhood and adolescence, she had search for that father and mother in the faces of the Shaker brothers and sisters and as dear as they were to her, she had never recognized them as her parents. It seemed an ungrateful thought at first but then she accepted it as a sorrow that was not to be denied. But she remembered that Shakers chose to be Shakers. They put on their Shaker dress with reverence to the lord and with a proud heart. It might be a lonely heart or a dejected heart, or a joyful one but the plain Shaker dress was of the same fabric each day.

The summer day now faded reluctantly and the grass in the fields turned to navy blue. The sky was orange along the horizon in a vanishing blue sky.

The following morning the trees in the yards came alive in the wind. A bright sunlight transmitted energy to all living things. The dark green leaves danced and lifted their bows to white clouds and a light blue sky above. The grass in the fields, too, came alive with movement from the strong wind. The air was cooler and from the North. It rolled down the grass-covered hills as if it had a life of its' own. As if independent of the sun and the other natural elements. The flowers and vegetables growing tall in the gardens, bowed, bent and swayed. The valley seemed more so that day; a lower more settled place between the green hills. The day would bring human activity like the wind, more forceful and decisive and it would shake this usually quiet Shaker place for the next weeks to follow. The strong wind caught the fabric of the Shaker sister's dresses and aprons and sent them rippling in the air. With squinting eyes and downturned mouths, they braved against the sudden gust carrying their garden baskets up to the pantry of the North Family house.

Inside the house and in the kitchen, Shaker Sister Clara made bread from sour dough she had prepared. It was a special Shaker recipe, simple but specific in its measurements of basic ingredients. The dough loaves were plump; her hands poking at the top edges of the sticky formed dough in the metal bread pans. She slid them into the heated oven to rise, bake and brown.

Cyryl had a dream the night before. It was of him and Rebecca dancing at their wedding. He was in his suit and she was wearing a white-lace dress with long, loose sleeves. She was no longer a Shaker woman but a woman of the world. There was music from a small violin orchestra. The floor was shellacked wood planks and there were others dancing around them as well. It might have been a fancy Greek restaurant. It was a sunny day but how he knew this he wasn't sure, as the dream took place indoors.

What Cyryl had learned as a young man was that life offers no expectations, only miracles or circumstances that rise above the mundane or ordinary. Courage and sheer human emotion, can bring one to voice what is not ordinarily expressed or demonstrated. What he had learned during his months at the Shaker village was that love had many ways of expressing itself. The gift of it to others the best reward. He had absorbed all of this like a good meal or a story told. There can be loneliness even in unity and the knowledge that one is loved. But the reassurance of love, in the face of great hardship, is a man or a woman's greatest strength. It fosters forgiveness and hope and the will to move

139

forward in all things, as life is to be lived day to day and year to year. With that knowledge of love, we can live and even die in peace.

Why was the sun orange that day? It was an ordinary day but there was the sun like an orange floating in the sky. The sky was a haze of white. It was one of those atmospheric wonders that occurred on occasion and could be explained only through scientific explanation that gave specifics of the chemicals and moisture content found in the air around us; numeric notes on a piece of paper.

The wind, birds, toads and insects made the noises you heard in the fields. It was the wind, though, that seemed closest to the idea and tone of human emotion. Time was measured by the pocket watch or chiming clock but also by the rise and fall of sunlight and the constant variation in temperature. But in fact, time was outside of any human estimate as it was god who ultimately measured time and what it represented. The low green hills of Appalachia had received a heavy rainfall from the previous day and night. The sun grew hot in the early morning hours; a sign of midsummer. There was a haze of clouds in the sky. Cyryl and Stephen worked together that day and they talked of the future.

"We should move on soon, but we don't have to just yet," said Cyryl.

"It's been a good start," said Stephen. "I hope we don't have bad luck or find ourselves poor and in a bad way somewhere."

"I think we will make out alright," said Cyryl.

Cyryl searched Stephen's face for any sign of fear or hesitation but he saw none. There was just a look of anticipation and contentment. Cyryl would never want to be the cause of Stephen's unhappiness. It was one of the reasons he was so confident. Things had to turn out well not only for Cyryl but for Stephen as well.

"We could find other work like this or a factory job. We should ask for a reference before we leave," said Stephen. "The farm deacon said we had done a good job. He was glad he had brought us on."

"We need our own place and a measure of freedom. Here, well, it seems as if we our living outside of society or in another," said Cyryl.

"It's a queer place but they have been good to us," said Stephen. "The food and lodging were good and the pay has allowed us to save some money."

140

XI

Indian Summer

It is that time of year when the remnants of summer remain and fall has yet to arrive. The green of summer remains. The sky is blue. No sign of the fall season gives alert to change. Flowers still bloom, green leaves cling to the trees and a hotter temperature defines an Indian summer. But from memory, you know that another fall season will appear and bring a gray sky and colorful falling leaves that dry and scatter in the stronger wind.

The mood of each season was assumed in the darker shadows of the Appalachian woods. Spring light with promise, Summer heavy with its' own element; fall for-telling the occult of evil or the chance for salvation and winter, waiting silently for a renewal.

It was now the beginning of the September month. Yet, the seasons seemed to transform into that one day. The orange and brown of fall was there in the shadows of the place. Winter was seen in brown and broken remnants of twigs and dust that covered the land under the trees. The spring season was left in the violets and budding wild-flowers and summer shown bright in the sky, in the sunlight beating down on the fields and making things grow more than the day before. A rural landscape view could be a window to another place, a wintery scene of snow drifts between the branches of trees, or a summer view of a wooded area covered in scattered sunlight. These were views that transcended the landscape and presented themselves as timeless, even metaphysical. You could choose to enter them or keep your distance in pursuit of another destination.

Cyryl stood outside of the men's residence for workmen. For a moment, he forgot where he was to go that day to do his work. He was thinking of the future. No one was there to tell him in which direction to go. But as he stood there he realized that he simply had to move ahead as he had before. He had found a home here. Home was a feeling certainly, but also a place to grow and learn. He had done that more than any other time in his life. The idea was to create something and to do it in the best way possible. Your materials should be the best from which to build.

There was never a morning when he was not willing to go to work, although he sometimes wished himself a man of leisure, if not for just one or two days; the purpose being an outing to a nearby lake or a trip into town. He might grow agitated by his work for the labor was hard at times and menial. He realized that it was the sort of work he would have to do on a farm. He would have to work hard at all sorts of things. Perhaps a factory job might be better but he knew he preferred working outdoors and at what he would consider his own labor, for his own purpose and not tied to someone else's industry.

The Shaker village could be a place of boredom, where stern individuals seemed to lack any sort of humor or lively thought; a place where God's work translated into hard work and extreme self-sacrifice. The idea of youth here seen as the measure of time you had known Christ the savior and how well that relationship had progressed. Not that children were not acknowledged as such, but always with this spiritual connection in mind. The severity of this place made you long for the urban activity of a town, regardless of its' size and the worldly conversation and dress of non-believers living a life of sin and pleasure. The memory of it made the Shakers seem narrow and unpleasant; conditioned to a hardship they had brought upon themselves. Some former Shaker members had left with this thought, of a sect too inflexible and at times, uncaring for the feelings and opinions of others who might hold a different perspective on the spiritual and a person's simple needs or human desires.

For Cyril and Stephen it was a temporary stay and knowing this made them more tolerant of their circumstances, but it also made them realize how they had developed as young men, having shared many of the same life experiences that had formed their characters; former sailors and fishermen, sons of immigrants and somehow outside of the normal pace and approval of a larger society that viewed them as inferior to what was aspired to and held as proper. It seemed fitting that they should find themselves with other human beings who too, were viewed by society as outside the norm of social practice and mode.

It was another afternoon of work in the fields. Cyryl and Stephen had taken shelter under a group of oak trees still dripping with rain. The rain started up again and this time with more force.

"You know that in ancient Greece there was a place in the center of the city called the Agora. It is where land owners would gather to hear words from the ruling king or government of that area. It was also a marketplace where items were sold and bought. This making and selling of Shaker goods made me think of it, I suppose," said Cyryl.

"Where did you learn that?" asked Stephen.

"From my papa," said Cyryl.

"I know a lot about ancient Greece," said Cyryl.

"You've told me some of it," said Stephen.

"Yes, that is true, I have told you some of the ancient Greek stories."

The two men did not speak for a few moments and listened to the falling rain.

"I am glad you decided to come with me," said Cyryl.

"We're best friends. I couldn't let you go off alone like that," said Stephen.

"We will always be first-rate friends I think," said Cyryl.

"It's pretty out here in Appalachia, as they call it. I like the rain," said Stephen.

"Rain always brings a stop to things. It forces you to stop and look up and around you," said Cyryl.

"You can't get much done when it rains. It forces you to think about things. Where will we go from here do you think?" asked Stephen.

"We'll move on to somewhere. We're better on land. We can make good lives for ourselves on land," said Cyryl.

"Well, I know one thing. I could never be a Shaker brother," said Stephen.

"Stephen, look at that" said Cyryl.

"What?" asked Stephen.

"The hills are a color of blue," said Cyryl.

143

"It's muddy woods. Bill told me those lower mountains were full of insects, snakes and possum," said Stephen.

There were flashes of lighting in the dark sky. There was the sound of distant thunder. The rain had let up some. The two made a run for it across the field towards the workmen's building to where the other workmen had retreated. There seemed to be a guiding force that had brought these two men together. A higher force they never seemed fully conscious of and if they had acknowledged, might have been described as of a spiritual kind. But they were aware that their daily actions and words reflected something between them that was from the origins of love and brotherhood. It seemed appropriate then that they had found another sort of brotherhood where they would thrive for a time.

The nearby mountains presented a physical barrier and yet, they stimulated the imagination as to what was beyond them. Cyryl and Stephen were beginning to wonder where they might find themselves beyond this Appalachian land area. They had not missed the city and this rural place had provided them a simpler way of life, unfettered and meaningful, in the most basic of ways.

XII

A Journey West

_____

As all dreams come to an end, some are remembered and some are not.
The Appalachian land once more faded into night shadows but before it did, the shape of the lower valley and surrounding hills held its colors of varied greens and shades of blue. The bright light of a sunset above the hills shimmered gold. That next morning a burst of sunlight brought another day to the Appalachian valley and hills. Soon it warmed the land. It looked and felt like a summer day always should; warm, bright and full of the deep colors of that season.

The sun rose to a cold morning; cold for a September day that would warm with the sun. Cyryl loaded the wagon to begin the journey. With their few belongings secure, his friend Stephen Blome ran alongside the wagon and jumped on. The Appalachian valley land on either side of them was a quilt of summer colors. The sky above them was picturesque and moody; gray clouds and blue sky. The weeds and flowers that bloomed alongside the road and open fields soon disappeared once the horse drawn wagon reached the narrow road through the woods. Cyryl shook the horse's reins to quicken its stride and he drove the wagon West.

The two men had set out for what would be a much longer journey than they had expected. They too, would become a part of the rebuilding of post, Civil War America.

Epilogue

One year, Stephen Blome and Cyryl Megalos went to New York City and visited the Statue of Liberty. They had a nice meal at a real Greek restaurant in lower Manhattan, not far from where Cyryl grew up. A man with a camera took their picture. They were both dressed in their best clothes.

The true magic of Appalachia could only allow for a happy ending to this American novel; not that the shadows don't give us an occasional *Rip Van Winkle* tale....

Suggested Reading

Francis, Richard. *Ann the Word, The Story of Ann Lee Female Messiah Mother of the Shakers. The Woman Clothed With The Sun.*

Arcade Publishing. 2013. Print.

Komanecky, Michael K. *The Shakers, From Mount Lebanon To The World.*

Skira Rizzoli. 2014. Print.

Stein, Stephen J. *The Shaker Experience In America. A History of the United Society of Believers.*

Yale University Press. 1992. Print.

Tassin, Susan Hutchison. *New York Ghost Towns, Uncovering The Hidden Past.*

Stackpole Books. 2013. Print.

Printed in the United States